Edge of Forever

**Center Point
Large Print**

Also by Sherryl Woods and available from Center Point Large Print:

Sean's Reckoning
Michael's Discovery
A Chesapeake Shores Christmas
Moonlight Cove
Beach Lane
An O'Brien Family Christmas

This Large Print Book carries the Seal of Approval of N.A.V.H.

Edge of Forever

SHERRYL WOODS

CENTER POINT LARGE PRINT
THORNDIKE, MAINE

This Center Point Large Print edition is published
in the year 2012 by arrangement with
Harlequin Books S.A.

The text of this Large Print edition is unabridged.
In other aspects, this book may
vary from the original edition.
Printed in the United States of America
on permanent paper.
Set in 16-point Times New Roman type.

ISBN: 978-1-61173-438-6

Library of Congress Cataloging-in-Publication Data

Woods, Sherryl.
Edge of forever / Sherryl Woods. — Large print ed.
p. cm. — (Center Point large print edition)
ISBN 978-1-61173-438-6 (library binding : alk. paper)
1. Large type books. I. Title.
PS3573.O6418E34 2012
813'.54—dc23
2012008671

Dear Friends,

Over the course of what now has become an amazingly long career, I've chosen most often to write about women who are survivors. That is certainly true of Dana Brantley, the heroine of *Edge of Forever*, one of my earliest books for Silhouette Special Edition. I'm absolutely delighted that her story is available again.

What do I mean by survivors? These are women who have faced almost insurmountable odds, a crisis so life-altering that many people would have given up. But not Dana Brantley, who has chosen to rebuild her life in a small riverfront community, hoping for anonymity while the wounds from her tragic past heal. Then along comes Nick Verone, whose attention threatens her hard-won serenity and whose love is almost sure to steal her heart. It's the story of a woman who's found the strength and courage to go on, and the man who's determined to stand beside her, no matter what.

I hope you'll find Dana's story both touching and inspiring, for the message I always want to communicate to you is that just beyond every dark corner, there is always hope.

All best,

Sherryl

Chapter 1

The lilac bush seemed as if it was about to swallow up the front steps. Its untamed boughs drooping heavily with fragile, dew-laden lavender blossoms, it filled the cool Saturday morning air with a glorious, sweet scent.

Dana Brantley, a lethal-looking pair of hedge clippers in her gloved hands, regarded the overgrown branches with dismay. Somewhere behind that bush was a small screened-in porch. With some strategic pruning, she could sit on that porch and watch storm clouds play tag down the Potomac River. She could watch silvery streaks of dawn shimmer on the smooth water. Those possibilities had been among the primary attractions of the house when she'd first seen it a few weeks earlier. Goodness knows, the place hadn't had many other obvious assets.

True, that enticing screened-in porch sagged; its weathered wooden planks had already been worn down by hundreds of sandy, bare feet. The yard was overgrown with weeds that reached as high as the few remaining upright boards in the picket fence. The cottage's dulled yellow paint was peeling, and the shutters tilted precariously. The air inside the four cluttered rooms was musty from years of disuse. The stove was an unreliable relic from another era, the refrigerator door hung loosely on one rusty hinge and the plumbing sputtered and groaned like an aging malcontent.

Despite all that, Dana had loved it on sight, with the same unreasoning affection that made one choose the sad-eyed runt in a litter of playful puppies. She especially liked the creaking wicker furniture with cushions covered in a fading flower print, the brass bed, even with its lumpy mattress, and the high-backed rocking chair on the front porch. After years of glass and chrome sterility, they were comfortable-looking in a delightfully shabby, well-used sort of way.

The real estate agent had apologized profusely for the condition of the place, had even suggested that they move on to other, more modern alternatives, but Dana had been too absorbed by the endless possibilities to heed the woman's urgings. Not only was the price right for her meager savings, but this was an abandoned house that could be slowly, lovingly restored and filled with light and sound. It would be a symbol of the life she was trying to put back together in a style far removed from that of her previous twenty-nine years. She knew it was a ridiculously sentimental attitude and she'd forced herself to act sensibly by making an absurdly low, very businesslike offer. To her amazement and deep-down delight it had been accepted with alacrity.

Dana turned now, cast a lingering look at the white-capped waves on the gray-green river and lifted the hedge clippers. She took a determined step toward the lilac bush, then made the mistake of inhaling deeply. She closed her eyes and sighed blissfully, then shrugged in resignation. She couldn't do it. She could not cut back one single branch. The pruning would simply have to wait until later, after the blooms faded.

In the meantime, she'd continue using the back door. At least she could get onto the porch from inside the house and her view wasn't entirely blocked. If she pulled the rocker to the far corner, she might be able to see a tiny sliver of the water and a glimpse of the Maryland shore on the opposite side. She'd probably catch a better breeze on the corner anyway, she thought optimistically. It was just one of the many small pleasures she had since leaving Manhattan and settling in Virginia.

River Glen was a quiet, sleepy town of seven thousand nestled along the Potomac. She'd visited a lot of places during her search for a job, but this one had drawn her in some indefinable way. With its endless stretches of green lawns and its mix of unpretentious, pastel-painted summer cottages, impressive old brick Colonial homes and modern ranch-style architecture, it was the antithesis of New York's intimidating mass of skyscrapers. It had a pace that soothed rather than grated and an atmosphere of unrelenting calm and continuity. The town, as much as the job offer, had convinced her this was exactly what she needed.

Four weeks earlier Dana had moved into her ramshackle cottage and the next day she'd started her job as River Glen's first librarian in five years. All in all, it had been a satisfying month with no regrets and no time for lingering memories.

Already she'd painted the cottage a sparkling white, scrubbed the layers of grime from the windows, matched wits with the stove and the plumbing and replaced the mattress. When she tired of being confined to the house, she had cut the overgrown lawn, weeded the flower gardens and discovered beds of tulips and daffodils ready to burst forth with blossoms. She'd even put in a small tomato patch in the backyard.

To her surprise, after a lifetime surrounded by concrete, she found that the scent of newly-turned earth, even the feel of the rich dirt clinging damply to her skin, had acted like a balm. Now, more than ever, she was glad she'd chosen springtime to settle here. All these growing things reminded her in a very graphic way of new beginnings.

"Better be careful," a low, distinctly sexy voice, laced with humor, warned from out of nowhere, startling Dana just as she reached out to pluck a lilac from the bush. She hadn't heard footsteps.

She certainly hadn't heard a car drive up. On guard, she whirled around, the clippers held out protectively in front of her, and discovered a blue pickup at the edge of the lawn, its owner grinning at her from behind the wheel.

"I heard that lilac bush ate the last owner," he added very seriously.

Her brown eyes narrowed watchfully. She instinctively backed up a step, then another as the stranger climbed out of his truck and started toward her with long, easy strides.

Dana had met a number of townspeople since her arrival, but not this man. She would have remembered the overpowering masculinity of the rugged, tanned face with its stubborn, square jaw and the laugh lines that spread like delicate webs from the corners of his eyes. She would have remembered the trembling nervousness he set off inside her.

"Who are you?" she asked, trying to hide her uneasiness but clinging defensively to the hedge clippers nonetheless. It was one thing to know the adage that in a small town there were no strangers, but quite another to be confronted unexpectedly with a virile, powerful specimen like this in your own front yard. She figured the hedge clippers made them an almost even match, which was both a reassuring and a daunting thought.

The man, tall and whipcord lean, paused halfway up the walk and shoved his hands into the pockets of his jeans. If he was taken aback by her unfriendliness, there was no sign of it on his face. His smile never wavered and his voice lowered to an even more soothing timbre, as if to prove he was no threat to her.

"Nicholas . . . Nick Verone." When that drew no response, he added, "Tony's father."

Dana drew in a sharp breath. The name, of course, had registered at once. It was plastered on the side of just about every construction trailer in the county. It was also the signature on her paycheck. She was a town employee. Nicholas Verone was the elected treasurer, a man reputed to have political aspirations on a far grander scale, perhaps the state legislature, perhaps even Washington.

He was admired for his integrity, respected for his success and, since the death of his wife three years earlier, targeted by every matchmaker in town. She'd been hearing about him since her first day on the job. Down at town hall, the kindly clerk, a gleam in her periwinkle-blue eyes, had taken one good look at Dana and begun scheming to arrange a meeting. To Betsy Markham's very evident maternal frustration, Dana had repeatedly declined.

The connection to Tony, however, was what mattered this morning. Turning her wary frown into a faint tentative smile of welcome, she saw the resemblance now, the same hazel eyes that

12

were bright and inquisitive and filled with warmth and humor, the same unruly brown hair that no brush would ever tame. While at ten years old Tony was an impish charmer, his father had a quiet, far more dangerous allure. The sigh of relief she'd felt on learning his identity caught somewhere in her throat and set off a different reaction entirely.

Ingrained caution and natural curiosity warred, making her tone abrupt as she asked, "What are you doing here?"

Nick Verone still didn't seem the least bit offended by her inhospitable attitude. In fact, he seemed amused by it. "Tony mentioned your roof was leaking. I had some time today and I thought maybe I could check it out for you."

Dana grimaced. She was going to have to remember to watch her tongue around Tony. She'd been alert to Betsy Markham's straightforward matchmaking tactics, but she'd never once suspected that Tony might decide to get in on the conspiracy to find his father a mate. Then again, maybe Tony had only been trying to repay her for helping him with his history lesson on the Civil War. At her urging, he'd finally decided not to try to persuade the teacher that the South had actually won.

"Well, we should have," he'd grumbled, his jaw set every bit as stubbornly as she imagined his father's could be. In the end, though, Tony had stuck to the facts and returned proudly a week later to show her the B minus on his test paper, the highest history grade he'd ever received.

At the moment, though, with Nick Verone waiting patiently in front of her, it hardly seemed to matter what Tony's motivation had been. She had to send the man on his way. His presence was making her palms sweat.

"Thanks, anyway," she said, giving him a smile she hoped seemed suitably appreciative. "But I've already made arrangements for a contractor to come by next week."

Instead of daunting him, her announcement drew a scowl. "I hope you didn't call Billy Watson."

Dana swallowed guiltily and said with a touch of defiance, "What if I did?"

"He'll charge you an arm and a leg and he won't get the job done."

"Haven't you heard that it's bad business to knock the competition?"

"Billy's not my competition. For that matter, calling him a contractor is a stretch of the imagination. He's a scoundrel out to make a quick buck so he can finance his next binge. Everybody around here knows that and I can't imagine anyone recommending him. Why did you call him in the first place?"

She'd called Billy Watson because he was the only *other* contractor—or handyman, for that matter—she'd been able to find when water had

14

started dripping through her roof in five different places during the first of April's pounding spring showers. All of Betsy's unsolicited praise for Nick Verone had set off warning bells inside her head. She'd known intuitively that asking him to take a look at her roof would be asking for trouble. His presence now and its impact on her heartbeat were proof enough that she'd been right. To any woman determinedly seeking solitude, this aggressive, incredibly sexy man was a threat.

She stared into Nick's eyes, noted the expectant gleam and decided that wasn't an explanation she should offer. He was the kind of man who'd make entirely too much out of such a candid response.

"You're a very busy man, Mr. Verone," she said instead. "I assumed Billy Watson could get here sooner."

Nick's grin widened, dipping slightly on the left side to make it beguilingly crooked. A less determined woman might fall for that smile, but Dana tried very hard to ignore it.

"I'm here now," he pointed out, rocking back and forth on the balls of his feet, his fingers still jammed into the pockets of his jeans in a way that called attention to their fit across his flat stomach and lean hips.

"Mr. Watson promised to be here Monday morning first thing. That's plenty soon enough."

"And if it rains between now and then?"

"I'll put out the pots and pans again."

Nick only barely resisted the urge to chuckle. He'd heard the dismissal in Dana's New York–accented voice and read the wariness in her eyes. It was the look a lot of people had when first confronted with small-town friendliness after a lifetime in big cities. They assumed every neighborly act would come with a price tag. It took time to convince them otherwise. Oddly enough, he found that in Dana's case he wanted to see to her enlightenment personally. There was something about this slender, overly-cautious woman that touched a responsive chord deep inside him.

Besides, he loved River Glen. He'd grown up here and he'd witnessed—in fact, he'd been a part of—its slow evolution from a slightly shabby summer resort past its prime into a year-round community with a future. The more people like Dana Brantley who settled here, the faster changes would come.

He'd read her résumé and knew that one year ago, at age twenty-eight, she'd gone back to school to finish her master's degree in library science. He was still a little puzzled why a native New Yorker would want to come to a quiet place like River Glen, but he was glad of it. She'd bring new ideas, maybe some big-city ways. He didn't want his town to lose its charm, but he wanted it to be progressive, rather than becoming mired down in the sea of complacency that had destroyed other communities and made their young people move on in search of more excitement.

He figured it was up to people in his position to see that Dana felt welcome. Small towns had a way of being friendly and clannish at the same time. Sometimes it took a while for superficial warmth to become genuine acceptance.

He gazed directly into Dana's eyes and shook his head. "Sorry, ma'am, it just wouldn't be right. I can't let you do that." He saw to it that his southern drawl increased perceptibly.

"Do what?" A puzzled frown tugged at her lips.

"Stay up all night, running from room to room with those pots and pans. What if you slipped and fell? I'd feel responsible."

The remark earned him a reluctant chuckle and he watched in awe at the transformation. Dana smiled provocatively, banishing the tiny, surprisingly stern lines in her lovely, heart-shaped face. She pulled off her work gloves and brushed back a curling strand of mink-brown hair that had escaped from her shoulder-length ponytail. Every movie cliché about staid librarians suddenly whipping off their glasses and letting down their hair rushed through Nick's mind and warmed his blood. Under all that starch and caution, under the streak of dirt that emphasized the curve of her cheek, Dana Brantley was a fragile, beautiful woman. The realization took his breath away. All Tony's talk hadn't done the new librarian justice.

"I swear to you that I won't sue you if I trip over a pot in the middle of a storm," she said. Her smile grew and, for the first time since his arrival, seemed sincere. Finally, she completely put aside the hedge clippers she'd been absentmindedly brandishing at him.

"I'll even put it in writing," she offered.

"Nope," he said determinedly. "That's not good enough. There's Tony to consider, too."

"What does he have to do with it?"

"Don't think I don't know that you're the one behind his history grade. I can't have him failing again just because the librarian is laid up with a twisted ankle or worse."

"Tony is a bright boy. All he needs is a little guidance." She regarded him pointedly. "And someone to remind him that when it comes to history, facts are facts. Like it or not, the Yankees did win the Civil War."

Nick hid a smile. "Yes, well, with Robert E. Lee having been born just down the road, some of us do like to cling to our illusions about that particular war. But for a battle here and there, things might have been different."

"But they weren't. However, if you're deter-mined to ignore historical reality, perhaps you should stick to helping Tony with his math or maybe his English and encourage him to read his history textbooks. In the long run, he'll have a better time of it in school."

Nick accepted the criticism gracefully, but there was a twinkle in his eyes. "I'll keep that in mind," he said, careful not to chuckle. "Now about your roof . . ."

"Mr. Verone—"

"Nick."

"That roof has been up there for years. It may have a few leaks, but it's in no danger of caving in. Surely it can wait until Monday. I appreciate your offering to help, but I did make a deal with Mr. Watson."

Nick was already moving toward his truck. "He won't show up," he muttered over his shoulder.

"What's that?"

"I said he won't show up, not unless he's out of liquor." He pulled an extension ladder from the back of the pickup and returned purposefully up the walk, past an increasingly indignant Dana.

"Mr. Verone," Dana snapped in frustration as Nick marched around to the side of the house. She had to run to keep up with him, leaving her out of breath but just as furious. The familiar, unpleasant feeling of losing control of a situation swept over her. "Mr. Verone, I do not want you on my roof."

It seemed rather a wasted comment since he was already more than halfway up the ladder.

Damn, she thought. *The man is impossible.* "Don't you ever listen?" she grumbled.

He climbed the rest of the way, then leaned down and winked at her. "Nope. Give me my toolbox, would you?"

She was tempted to throw it at him, but she handed it up very politely, then sat down on the back step muttering curses. She picked a blade of grass and chewed on it absentmindedly. With Nick Verone on her roof and a knot forming in her stomach, she was beginning to regret that she'd ever helped Tony Verone with his history project. In fact, she was beginning to wonder if coming to River Glen was going to be the peaceful escape she'd hoped it would be. Sensations best forgotten were sweeping over her this morning.

While she tried to put her feelings in perspective, Nick shouted at her from some spot on the roof she couldn't see.

"Do you have a garden hose?"

"Of course."

"How about getting it and squirting some water up here?"

Dana wanted to refuse but realized that being difficult probably wouldn't get Nick out of her life any faster. He'd just climb down and find the hose himself. He seemed like a very resourceful man. She stomped off after the hose and turned it on.

"Aim it a little higher," he instructed a few minutes later. "Over here."

Dana scowled up at him and fought the temptation to move the spray about three feet to the right and douse the outrageous, arrogant man. Maybe then he would go away, even if only to get into some dry clothes, but at least he'd leave her in peace for a while. She still wasn't exactly sure how he'd talked her into letting him stay on the roof, much less gotten her to help him with his inspection. For a total stranger he took an awful lot for granted. He certainly didn't know how to take no for an answer. And she was tired of fighting, tired of confrontations and still, despite the past year of relative calm, terrified of anger. A raised voice made her hands tremble and her head pound with seemingly irrational anxiety.

So, if it made him happy, Nick Verone could inspect her roof, fix her leaks, and then, with any luck, he'd disappear and she'd be alone again. Blissfully alone with her books and her herb tea and her flowers, like some maiden aunt in an English novel.

Suddenly a tanned face appeared at the edge of the roof. "I hate to tell you this, but you ought to replace the whole thing. It's probably been up here thirty years without a single repair. I can patch it for you, but with one good storm, you'll just have more leaks."

Dana sighed. "Somehow I knew you were going to say that."

"Didn't you have the roof inspected before you bought the place?"

"Not exactly."

He grinned at her. "What does that mean?"

"It means we all agreed it was probably in terrible condition and knocked another couple of thousand dollars off the price of the house." She shot him a challenging glance. "I thought it was a good deal."

"I see." His eyes twinkled in that superior I-should-have-known male way and her hackles rose. If he said one word about being penny-wise and pound-foolish, she'd snatch the ladder away and leave him stranded.

Perhaps he sensed her intention, because he scrambled for the ladder and made his way down. When he reached the ground, he faced her, hands on hips, one foot propped on the ladder's lower rung in a pose that emphasized his masculinity.

"How about a deal?" he suggested.

Dana was shaking her head before the words were out of his mouth. "I don't think so."

"You haven't even heard the offer yet."

"I appreciate your interest and your time, Mr. Verone . . ."

"Nick."

She scowled at him. "But as I told you, I do have another contractor coming."

"Billy Watson will tell you the same thing, assuming he doesn't poke his clumsy feet through some of the weak spots and sue you first."

"Don't you think you're exaggerating slightly?"

"Not by much," he insisted ominously. Then he smiled again, one of those crooked, impish smiles that were so like Tony's when he knew he'd written something really terrific and was awaiting praise. Like father, like son—unfortunately, in this case.

"Why don't we go inside and have something cold to drink and discuss this?" Nick suggested, taking over again in a way that set Dana's teeth on edge. Her patience and self-control were deteriorating rapidly.

He was already heading around the side of the house before she even had a chance to say no. Once more, she was left to scamper along behind him or be left cursing to herself. At the back door she hesitated, not at all sure she wanted to be alone with this stranger and out of sight of the neighbors.

He's Tony's father, for heaven's sakes.

With that thought in mind, she stepped into the kitchen, but she lingered near the door. Nick hadn't waited for an invitation. He'd already opened the refrigerator and was scanning the contents with unabashed interest. He pulled out a pitcher of iced tea and poured two glasses without so much as a glance in her direction. To his credit, though, he didn't mention the fact that the door was missing a hinge. She'd ordered it on Thursday.

Nick studied Dana over the rim of his glass and tried to make sense of her skittishness. She was no youngster, though she had the trim, lithe figure of one. The weariness around her eyes was what gave her age away, not the long, slender legs shown off by her paint-splattered shorts or the luxuriant tumble of rich brown hair hanging down her back. Allowing for gaps in her résumé, she was no more than twenty-nine, maybe thirty, about five years younger than he was. Yet in some ways she looked as though she'd seen the troubles of a woman twice that age. There was something about her eyes, something sad and lost and vulnerable. Still, he didn't doubt for an instant that she had a core of steel. He'd felt the chill when her voice turned cold, when those intriguing brown eyes of hers glinted with anger. He'd pushed her this morning and she'd bent, but she hadn't broken. She was still fighting mad. Right now, she was watching him with an uneasy alertness, like a doe standing at the edge of a clearing and sensing danger.

"Now about that deal," he said when he'd taken a long swallow of the sweetened tea.

"Mr. Verone, please."

"Nick," he automatically corrected again. "Now what I have in mind is charging you just for the roofing materials. I'll handle the work in my spare time, if you'll continue to help Tony out with his homework."

Dana sighed, plainly exasperated with him. "I'm more than willing to help Tony anytime he asks for help. That's part of my job as librarian."

"Is it part of your job to stay overtime? I've seen the lights burning in there past closing more than once. We don't pay for the extra hours."

"I'm not asking you to. I enjoy what I do. I'm not interested in punching a time clock. If staying late will give someone extra time to get the books they want or to finish a school project, it gives me satisfaction."

"Okay, so helping Tony is part of your job. Then we'll just consider this my way of welcoming you to town."

"I can't let you do that," she insisted, her annoyance showing again.

"Why not? Don't tell me you're from that old-fashioned school that says women can't accept gifts from men unless they're engaged."

"I don't think fixing my roof is in the same league as accepting a fur coat or jewelry."

"Then I rest my case."

"But I will feel obligated to you and I don't like obligations."

"You won't owe me a thing. It's an even trade."

Dana groaned. "Is there any way I can win this argument?"

"None that I can think of," he admitted cheerfully.

"Okay, fine. Fix the roof," she said, but she

didn't sound pleased about it. She sounded like a woman who'd been cornered. For some reason, Nick felt like a heel instead of a good neighbor, though he couldn't find any logical explanation for her behavior or his uncomfortable reaction.

Changing tactics, he finally asked, "How come I haven't seen much of you around town?"

"I've been pretty busy getting settled in. This place was a mess and I had the library to organize."

He tilted his chair back on two legs and glanced around approvingly. "You've done a lot here. I remember the way it was. I used to play here as a boy when old Miss Francis was alive. It didn't look much better then. We thought it was haunted."

He was rewarded with another grin from Dana. "I haven't encountered any ghosts so far. If they're here, they certainly haven't done much of the cleaning. The library wasn't any improvement. It took me the better part of a week just to sweep away the cobwebs and organize the shelves properly. There are still boxes of donated books in the back I haven't had a chance to look at yet."

"Then it's time you took a break. There's bingo tonight at the fire station. Why don't you come with Tony and me?"

He watched as the wall around her went right back up, brick by brick. "I don't think so."

"Can't you spell?" he teased.

Her eyes flashed dangerous sparks. "Of course."

"How about counting? Any good at that?"

"Yes."

"Then what's the problem?"

The problem, Dana thought, was not bingo. It was Nicholas Verone. He represented more than a mere complication, more than a man who wanted to fix her roof and share a glass of tea now and then. He was the type of man she'd sworn to avoid for the rest of her life. Powerful. Domineering. Charming. And from the glint in his devilish eyes to the strength in his work-roughened hands he was thoroughly, unquestionably male. Just looking at those hands, imagining their strength, set off a violent trembling inside her.

"Thank you for asking," she said stiffly, "but I really have too much to do. Maybe another time."

To her astonishment, Nick's eyes sparked with satisfaction. "Next week, then," he said as he rinsed his glass and set it in the dish drainer. He didn't once meet her startled gaze.

"But—" The protest might as well never have been uttered for all the good it did. He didn't even allow her to finish it.

"We'll pick you up at six and we'll go out for barbecue first," he added confidently as he walked to the door, then bestowed a dazzling smile on her. "Gracie's has the best you've ever tasted this side of Texas. Guaranteed."

The screen door shut behind him with an emphatic bang.

27

Dana watched him go and fought the confusing, contradictory feelings he'd roused in her. If there was one thing she knew all too well, it was that there were no guarantees in life, especially when it came to men like Nick Verone.

Chapter 2

After a perfectly infuriating Monday morning spent waiting futilely for Billy Watson, Dana opened the library at noon. She'd found Betsy Markham already pacing on the front steps. Instead of heading for the fiction shelves to look over her favorite mysteries, Betsy followed Dana straight to her cluttered desk, where she was trying to update the chaotic card file so she could eventually get it all on the computer. The last librarian, a retired cashier from the old five-and-ten-cent store, obviously hadn't put much stock in the need for alphabetical order or modern equipment. When a new book came in, she apparently just popped the card in the back of whichever drawer seemed to have room.

"So," Betsy said, pulling up a chair and propping her plump elbows on the corner of the desk. "Tell me everything."

Dana glanced up from the card file and stared at her blankly. "About what?"

"You and Nick Verone, of course." She wagged a finger. "You're a sly little thing, Dana Brantley. Here I've been trying to introduce you to the man for weeks and you kept turning me down. The next thing I know the two of you are thick as thieves and being talked about all over town."

Thick brown brows rose over startled eyes. "We're what?"

"Yes, indeed," Betsy said, nodding so hard that not even the thick coating of hair spray could contain the bounce of her upswept gray hair.

Betsy's eyes flashed conspiratorially and she lowered her voice, though there wasn't another soul in the place. "Word is that he was at your house very early Saturday morning and stayed for quite a while. One version has it he was there till practically lunchtime. Inside the house!"

When she noticed the horrified expression on Dana's face, she added, "Though what difference that makes, I for one can't see. It's not as if you'd be doing anything in broad daylight."

Dana was torn between indignation and astonishment. "He didn't stop by for some sort of secret assignation, for heaven's sakes. He came to look at my roof."

Betsy appeared taken aback. "But I thought you'd called Billy Watson to do that, even though I tried to make it perfectly clear to you that Billy's a bit of a ne'er-do-well."

"I had called him, and don't get me started on

that. The man never showed up this morning. He said he'd be there by eight. I waited until 11:30." Dana wasn't sure what incensed her more: Billy Watson's failure to appear or having to admit that Nick Verone was right.

"Then I still don't understand what Nick has to do with your roof."

"Mr. Verone apparently heard about the leaks from Tony and stopped by on his own. He wasn't invited." Darn! Why was she explaining herself to Betsy Markham and, no doubt, half the town by sunset? Nick's visit had been entirely innocent. On top of that, it was no one's business.

Except in River Glen.

She'd have to start remembering that this wasn't New York, where all sorts of mayhem could take place right under your neighbors' noses without a sign of acknowledgment. Here folks obviously took their gossip seriously. She decided that Crime Watch organizers could take lessons from the citizens of this town. Very little got by them. Perhaps she should be grateful they hadn't prayed for her soul in the Baptist church on Sunday or put an announcement in the weekly paper.

Betsy was staring at her, disappointment etched all over her round face. "You mean there's nothing personal going on between the two of you?"

Dana thought about the invitation to bingo. That was friendly, not personal, but she doubted Betsy and the others would see it that way. She might as well bring it up now, rather than wait for Saturday night, when half the town was bound to see her with Nick and Tony and the rest would hear about it before church the next day. "Not exactly," she said finally.

Betsy's blue eyes brightened. "I knew it," she gloated. "I just knew the two of you would hit it off. When are you seeing him again?"

"Saturday," Dana admitted reluctantly, then threw in what she suspected would be a wasted disclaimer, "but it's not really a date."

Betsy regarded her skeptically, just as Dana had known she would. Dana forged on anyway. "He and Tony and I are going out to eat at some place called Gracie's and then to bingo."

She thought that certainly ought to seem innocuous enough. Betsy reacted, though, as if Dana had uttered a blasphemy. She was incredulous.

"Barbecue and bingo? Land sakes, girl, Nick Verone's nigh on to the richest man in these parts. He ought to be taking you to someplace fancy in Richmond at the very least."

"I think the idea is for me to get to know more people around here. I don't think he's trying to woo me with gourmet food and candlelight."

"Then he's a fool."

Dana doubted if many people called Nick Verone a fool to his face. But Betsy had taken a proprietary interest in Dana's social life. She

31

might do it out of some misguided sense of duty.

"Don't you say one single word to him, Betsy Markham," she warned. "Barbecue and bingo are fine. I'm not looking for a man in my life—rich or poor. To tell the truth, I'd rather stay home and read a good book."

"You read books all day long. You're young. You ought to be out enjoying yourself, living life, not just reading about it in some novel."

"I do enjoy myself."

Betsy sniffed indignantly. "I declare, I don't know what's wrong with young people today. When my Harry and I were courting, you can bet we didn't spent Saturday night at the fire station with a bunch of nosy neighbors looking on. It's bad enough we do that now. Back then, why, we'd be parked out along the beach someplace, watching the moon come up and making plans."

She picked up a flyer from Dana's desk and fanned herself absentmindedly. There was a faint smile on her lips. "Oh, my, yes. That was quite a time. You young folks don't care a thing about romance. Everybody's too busy trying to get ahead."

Dana restrained the urge to grin. Being River Glen's librarian was hardly a sign of raging ambition, but if thinking it kept Betsy from interfering in her personal life, she'd do everything she could to promote the notion.

Dana reached over and patted the woman's

32

hand. "Thanks for caring about me, Betsy, but I'm doing just fine. I love it here. All I want in my life right now is a little peace and quiet. Romance can wait."

Betsy sighed dramatically. "Okay, honey, if that's what you want, but don't put up too much of a fight. Nick Verone's the best catch around these parts. You'd be crazy to let him get away."

Dana spent the rest of the afternoon thinking about Betsy's admonition. She also spent entirely too much time thinking about Nick Verone. Even if her mind hadn't betrayed her by dredging up provocative images, there was Tony to remind her.

He bounded into the library right after school, wearing a huge grin. "Hey, Ms. Brantley, I hear you and me and Dad are going out on Saturday."

Dana winced as several other kids turned to listen. "Your dad invited me to come along to bingo. Are you sure you don't mind?"

"Mind? Heck, no. You're the greatest. All the kids think so. Right, guys?" There were enthusiastic nods from the trio gathered behind him. Tony studied her with an expression that was entirely too wise for a ten-year-old and lowered his voice to what he obviously considered to be a discreet whisper. It echoed through every nook and cranny in the library.

"Say, do you want me to get lost on Saturday night?" He blushed furiously as his friends moved in closer so they wouldn't miss a word. "I mean so you and Dad can be alone and all. I could spend the night over at Bobby's. His mom wouldn't mind." Bobby nodded enthusiastically.

If Dana had been the type, she might have blushed right along with Tony. Instead, she said with heartfelt conviction, "I most certainly do not want you to get lost. Your father planned for all of us to spend the evening together and that's just the way I want it."

"But I know about grown-ups and stuff. I don't want to get in the way. I think it'd be great, if you and Dad—"

"Tony!"

"Well, you know."

"What I know," she said briskly, "is that you guys have an English assignment due this week. Have you picked out your books yet?"

All of them except Tony said yes and drifted off. Tony's round hazel eyes stared at her hopefully. "I thought maybe you'd help me."

Dana sighed. She knew now where Tony had gotten his manipulative skills. He was every bit as persuasive as his daddy. She pulled *Robinson Crusoe*, *Huckleberry Finn* and *Treasure Island* from the shelves. "Take a look at these."

She left him skimming through the books and went to help several other students who'd come in with assignments. The rest of the afternoon and evening flew by. At nine o'clock, when she was ready to lock up for the day, she discovered that

Tony was in a back corner still hunched over *Treasure Island*.

"Tony, you should have been home hours ago," she said in dismay. "Your father must be worried sick."

He barely glanced up at her. "I called him and told him where I was. He said it was okay."

"When did you call him?"

"After school."

Dana groaned. "Do you have any idea how late it is now?"

He shook his head. "Nope. I got to reading this. It's pretty good."

"Then why don't you check it out and take it home with you?"

He regarded her sheepishly. "I'd rather read it here with you."

An unexpected warm feeling stole into her heart. She could understand how Tony felt. He'd probably gone home all too often to an empty house. He'd clearly been starved for mothering since his own mother had died, despite the attentions of a maternal grandmother he mentioned frequently and affectionately. Whatever women there were in Nick Verone's life, they weren't meeting Tony's needs. A disturbing glimmer of satisfaction rippled through her at that thought, and she mentally stomped it right back into oblivion, where it belonged. The Verones' lifestyle was none of her concern.

Knowing that and acting on it, however, were two very different things. Subconsciously she'd felt herself slipping into a nurturing role with Tony from the day they'd met. Despite his boundless energy, there had been something a little lost and lonely about him. He reminded her of the way she'd felt for far too long, and instinctively she'd wanted to banish the sad expression from his eyes.

For Dana, Tony had filled an aching emptiness that increasingly seemed to haunt her now that she knew it was never likely to go away. From the time she'd been a little girl, her room cluttered with dolls in every shape and size, she'd wanted children of her own. She'd had a golden life in which all her dreams seemed to be granted, and she'd expected that to be the easiest wish of all to fulfill.

When she and Sam had married, they'd had their lives planned out: a year together to settle in, then a baby and two years after that another one. But too many things had changed in that first year, and ironically, she'd been the one to postpone getting pregnant, even though the decision had torn her apart.

Now her marriage was over and she wasn't counting on another one. She didn't even want one. And it was getting late. She was nearing the age when a woman began to realize it was now or never for a baby. She'd forced herself to accept the fact that for her it would be never, but there were still days when she longed for that child to hold in her empty arms. Tony, so hungry for attention, had seemed to be a godsend, but she knew now that her instinctive nurturing had to stop. It wasn't healthy for Tony and it assuredly wasn't wise for her—not with Nick beginning to hint around that it might be a package deal.

"Get your stuff together," she said abruptly to Tony. "I'll drive you home."

Hurt sprang up in his eyes at her sharp tone.

"I can walk," he protested with the automatic cockiness of a young boy anxious to prove himself grown up. Then his eyes lit up. "But if you drive me home," he said slyly, "maybe you can come in and have some ice cream with dad and me."

"Ice cream is not a proper dinner," Dana replied automatically, and then could have bitten her outspoken tongue.

"Yeah, but Dad's a pretty lousy cook. We go to Gracie's a lot. When we don't go there, we usually eat some yucky frozen dinners. I'd rather have ice cream."

Dana felt a stirring of something that felt disturbingly like sympathy as she pictured Nick and Tony existing on tasteless dinners that came in little metal trays. If these images kept up, she was going to have to buy army boots to stomp them out. The Verones' diet was of absolutely no concern to her. Tony looked sturdy enough and Nick was certainly not suffering from a lack of vitamins. She'd seen his muscle tone for herself, when he'd been stretching around up on her roof.

"So, how about it?" Tony said, interrupting her before she got lost in those intriguing images again. "Will you come in for ice cream?"

"Not tonight." Not in this lifetime, if she had a grain of sense in her head. She tried to ignore the disappointment that shadowed Tony's face as he gave her directions to his house.

It took less than ten minutes to drive across town to an area where the homes were separated by wide sweeps of lawn shaded by ancient oak trees tipped with new green leaves. The Verones' two-story white frame house, with its black shutters, wraparound porch and upstairs widow's walk, stood atop a low rise and faced out to sea. The place appeared to have been built in fits and starts, with additions jutting out haphazardly, yet looking very much a part of the whole. Lights blinked in the downstairs windows and an old-fashioned lamppost lit the driveway that wound along the side of the house. More than three times as large as Dana's two-bedroom cottage, the place still had a warm, cozily inviting appeal.

She was still absorbing that satisfying first impression when the side door opened and Nick appeared. Tony threw open the car door and jumped out. "Hey, Dad, Ms. Brantley brought me home. I asked her to come in for ice cream, but she won't. You try."

Dana wondered if she could disappear under the dashboard. Before she could attempt that feat, Nick was beside the car, an all-too-beguiling grin on his face. He leaned down and poked his head in the window. His hair was still damp from a recent shower and he smelled of soap. Dana tried not to sigh. She avoided his gaze altogether.

"How about it, Ms. Brantley?" he said quietly, drawing her attention. "Will I have any better luck than Tony?"

She caught the challenge glinting in his hazel eyes and looked away. "It's late. I really should be getting home and Tony ought to have some dinner."

"You both ought to have dinner," Nick corrected. "I'll bet you haven't eaten, either."

"I'll grab something at home. Thanks, anyway."

She risked glancing up. Nick tried for a woebegone expression and failed miserably. The man would look self-confident trying to hold back an avalanche single-handedly. "You wouldn't sentence Tony to another one of my disastrous meals, would you?"

Despite her best intentions, Dana found herself returning his mischievous grin. "Surely you're not suggesting that I stay for dinner and that I fix it."

His eyes widened innocently. On Tony it would

have been the look of an angel. On Nick it was pure seduction. "Of course not," he denied. "I'll just pop another TV dinner in the oven. We have plenty."

Suddenly she knew the battle was over before it had even begun. If Nick had been by himself, she would have refused; her defenses would have held. He would have been eating some prepackaged dinner, while she went home to canned vegetable soup and a grilled cheese sandwich. The idea of being alone with him made her heart race in a disconcerting way that would have made it easy to say no, even when the alternative wasn't especially appealing.

But with Tony around, she began to waver. He needed a nourishing meal. And while a ten-year-old, especially one who already had match-making skills, was hardly a qualified chaperon, he was better than nothing. She wouldn't have to be there more than an hour or so. How much could happen between them in a single hour?

"Do you have any real food in there?" she asked at last.

"Frozen dinners are real food."

"I was thinking more along the lines of chicken or beef or fish. This town has a river full of perch and crabs. Surely you occasionally go out and catch some of them."

"Of course I do. Then we eat them. I think there might be some chicken in the freezer, though."

"And vegetables?"

"Sure." Then as an afterthought, he added, "Frozen."

Dana shook her head. "Men!"

Telling herself it might be nice to have a friend in town, then telling herself she was an idiot for thinking that's all it would be with a man like Nick, she reluctantly turned off the ignition and climbed out of the car. "Guide me to your refrigerator. We'll consider this payment for your first day's labor on my roof."

"So Billy didn't show up?" he said, jamming his hands in his pockets.

She scowled at him. "No."

"I told—"

"Don't you dare finish that sentence."

"Right," he said agreeably, but his grin was very smug as he turned away to lead her up the driveway.

If she'd thought for one minute that she'd be able to relax in Nick's presence, she was wrong. Her nerves were stretched taut simply by walking beside him to the house. He didn't put a hand on her, not even a casual touch at her elbow to guide her. But every inch of her was vibrantly aware of him just the same and every inch screamed that this attempt at casual friendship was a mistake. At the threshold, she had to fight against a momentary panic, a desire to turn and flee, but then Tony was calling out to her and

41

curiosity won out over fear. She told herself she simply wanted to see if this graceful old house was as charming on the inside as it was outside.

In some ways the house itself had surprised her. She would have expected a builder to want something modern, something that would make a statement about his professional capabilities. Instead, Nick had chosen tradition and history. It raised him a notch in her estimation.

They went through the kitchen, which was as modern and large as anyone could possibly want. She regarded it enviously and thought of her own cantankerous appliances. A built-in breakfast nook was surrounded by panes of beveled glass and situated to catch the morning sun. This room was made for more than cooking and eating. It was a place for sharing the day's events, for making plans and shaping dreams, for watching the change of seasons. It was exactly the sort of kitchen she would have designed if she and Sam had ever gotten around to building a house.

Enough of that, she told herself sharply. She dropped her purse on the gleaming countertop and headed straight for the refrigerator. Nick stepped in front of her so quickly she almost stumbled straight into his arms. She pulled back abruptly to avoid the contact.

"Hey, don't you want the grand tour first?" Nick said. "I really didn't invite you in just to feed us. Relax for a while and let me show you around."

Once more, with her heart thumping crazily in her chest, Dana prayed for a quick return of her common sense. She knew she was feeling pressure where there was none, but suddenly she didn't want to see the rest of the house. She didn't want to find that the living room was as perfect as the one she'd dreamed about for years or that the bedrooms were bright and airy like something straight out of a decorating magazine. She didn't want to be here at all. Nick was too overwhelming, too charming, and there was an appreciative spark in his eyes that terrified her more with every instant she spent in his company.

She took a deep, slow breath and reminded herself that leaving now was impossible without seeming both foolish and ungracious. She took another calming breath and tried to remind herself that she was in control, that nothing would happen unless she wanted it to, certainly not with Tony in the house. Unfortunately, Tony seemed to have vanished the minute they came through the door. If only he'd join them, she might feel more at ease.

"Let me see what treasures are locked in your freezer first," she finally said. "Then while dinner cooks, you can show me around."

It was a logical suggestion, one that didn't hint of her absurd nervousness, and Nick gave in easily. "How about a drink, then?"

Once again, Dana felt a familiar knot form in

her stomach. "Nothing for me, thanks." Her voice was tight.

"Not even iced tea or a soda?"

Illogical relief, exaggerated far beyond the offer's significance, washed over her. "Iced tea would be great."

They reached the refrigerator at the same instant and Dana was trapped between Nick and the door. The intimate, yet innocent press of his solid, very male body against hers set off a wild trembling. His heat and that alluring scent of soap and man surrounded her. The surge of her blood roared in her ears. She clenched her fists and fought to remain absolutely still, to not let the unwarranted panic show in her eyes. Nick allowed the contact to last no more than a few seconds, though it seemed an eternity. Then he stepped aside with an easy grin.

"Sorry," he said.

Dana shrugged. "No problem."

But there was a problem. Nick had seen it in Dana's eyes, though she'd looked away to avoid his penetrating gaze. He'd felt the shiver that rippled through her, noted her startled gasp and the way she protectively lifted her arms before she dropped them back to her sides with conscious deliberation. He was experienced enough to know that this was not the reaction of a woman who desired a man but who was startled by the unexpectedness of the feeling. Dana had actually seemed afraid of him, just as she had on Saturday, when she'd been brandishing those hedge clippers. The possibility that he frightened her astonished and worried him. He was not used to being considered a threat, not to his employees, not to his son and certainly not to a woman.

He'd been raised to treat everyone with respect and dignity, but women were in a class by themselves. His mother, God rest her, had been a gentle soul with a core of iron and more love and compassion than any human being he'd ever met. She'd expected to be treated like a lady by both her husband and her sons and thought there was no reason other women shouldn't deserve the same.

"Women aren't playthings," she'd told Nick sternly the first time she'd caught him kissing a girl down by the river. He'd been fourteen at the time and very much interested in experimentation. Nancy Ann had the reputation of being more than willing. He never knew for sure if his mother had heard the gossip about Nancy Ann, but she'd looked him straight in the eye at the dinner table that night and said, "I don't care who they are or how experienced they claim to be, you show them the same respect you'd expect for yourself. Nobody deserves to be used."

Though his brothers had grinned, he'd squirmed uncomfortably under her disapproving gaze. He'd never once forgotten that lesson, not even in

45

the past three years since Ginny had died and more than a few women had indicated their willingness to share his bed and his life. Dana's nervous response bothered him all the more, because he knew it was so thoroughly unjustified.

But *she* didn't know that, he reminded himself. Experience had apparently taught her another lesson about men, a bitter, lasting lesson. He felt an unreasoning surge of anger against the person who had hurt her.

Dana was already poking around in the freezer as if the incident had never taken place. Since she'd apparently decided to let the matter rest, he figured he should, as well. For now. In time, his actions would teach her she had nothing to fear from him.

Delighted to have such attractive company for a change, he leaned back against the counter, crossed his legs at the ankles and watched her as she picked up packages, wrinkled her nose and tossed them back. Finally she emerged triumphant, her cheeks flushed from the chilly air in the freezer.

"I'm almost afraid to ask, but do you have any idea how long this chicken has been in there?"

Nick reached out, took the package and brushed at the frost. "Looks to me like it's dated February something."

"Of what year?"

"It's frozen. Does it matter?"

"Probably not to the chicken, but it could make a difference in whether we survive this meal."

"We can always go back to the frozen dinners. I bought most of them last week." He paused thoughtfully. "Except for those Salisbury steak things. They've probably been there longer. Tony said if I ever made him eat another one he'd report me to his grandmother for feeding him sawdust."

The comment earned a full-blown, dazzling smile and Nick felt as though he'd been granted an award. Whatever nervousness Dana had been feeling seemed to be disappearing now that she had familiar tasks to do. She moved around the kitchen efficiently, asking for pans and utensils as she needed them. In less than half an hour, there were delicious aromas wafting from the stove.

"What are you making?"

"Coq au vin. Now," she said, "if you'll point out the dishes and silverware, I'll set the table."

"No, you won't. That's Tony's job. We'll take our tour now and send him in."

Nick anxiously watched the play of expressions on Dana's face as he led her through the downstairs of the house. For a man who'd never given a hang what anyone thought, he desperately wanted her approval. The realization surprised him. He held his breath until she exclaimed over the gleaming wide-plank wooden floors, the antiques that he and Ginny had chosen with such care, the huge fireplace that was cold now but had warmed many a winter night. The beveled mirror in a huge oak cabinet caught the sparkle in Dana's huge brown eyes as she ran her fingers lovingly over the intricate carving.

As they wandered, Missy, a haughty Siamese cat that belonged to no one but deigned to live with Nick, regarded them cautiously from her perch on the windowsill. Finally, she stood up and stretched lazily. To Nick's astonishment, the cat then jumped down and rubbed her head on Dana's ankle. Dana knelt down and scratched the cat under her chin, setting off a loud purring.

"That's amazing," Nick said. "Missy is not fond of people. She loved Ginny, but she barely tolerates me and Tony. Usually she ignores strangers."

"Perhaps she's just very selective," Dana retorted with a lift of one brow. "A wise woman is always discriminating."

"Is there a message in there for me?"

"Possibly." There was a surprising twinkle in her eyes when she said it.

"You wouldn't be trying to warn me away, would you?" he inquired lightly. "Because if you are, let me tell you something: I don't give up easily on the things I value."

Dana swallowed nervously, but it was the only hint she gave of her nervousness. She met his gaze steadily as she gracefully stood up after giving Missy a final pat.

Tension filled the air with an unending silence that strummed across Nick's nerves. Flames curled inside and sent heat surging through him. Desire swept over him with a power that was virtually irresistible. For the first time in years he recalled the intensity of unfulfilled passion, the need that could drive all other thoughts from your mind. He gazed at Dana and felt that aching need. Dana, so determinedly prim and proper in her severely tailored brown skirt and plain beige silk blouse, was every inch a classy lady, but she stirred a restless, wild yearning inside him.

It was Dana who broke the nerve-racking silence.

"You can't lose what you don't have," she said very, very quietly before moving on to the next room. Left off balance by the comment, Nick stayed behind for several minutes trying to gather his wits and calm his racing pulse.

By the time they found Tony, it was time to serve dinner. There was no time for a complete tour of the bedrooms. It was probably just as well, Nick told himself. The sight of Dana standing anywhere near his bed might have driven him to madness.

What caused this odd, insistent pull he felt toward her? Certainly it was more than her luxuriant hair and wide eyes, more than her long-limbed grace. Was it the vulnerability that lurked beneath the surface? Or was it as elusive as the sense that, for whatever reason, she was forbidden, out of reach? He'd been with her twice now, but he knew little more about her than the facts she'd put on her résumé. She talked, even joked, but revealed nothing. He wanted much more. He wanted to know what went on in her head, what made her laugh and why she cried. He wanted to discover everything there was to know about Dana Brantley.

Most infuriating of all to a man of his methodical, cautious ways, he didn't know why.

During dinner, Tony chattered away, basking in Dana's quiet attention, and Nick tried to puzzle out the attraction. Soon though, the talk and laughter drew him in and he left the answers for another day.

Saturday. Only five days and he would have another chance to discover the mysterious allure she held for him. Five days that, in his sudden impatience, yawned before him like an eternity.

Chapter 3

Dana spent the rest of the week thinking up excuses to get her out of Saturday night's date. None was as irrefutable—or as factual—as simply telling Nick quite firmly: *I don't want to go.* Unfortunately, each time she looked into Tony's excited eyes, she couldn't get those harsh words past her lips.

She searched for a word to describe the tumult she'd felt after her visit to Nick's place. Disquieting. That was it. Nick had been a gentleman, the perfect host. On the surface their conversational banter had been light, but there had been sensual undercurrents so swift that at times she had felt she'd be caught up and swept away. Nick's brand of gentle attentiveness spun a dangerous web that could hold the most unwilling woman captive until the seduction was complete.

Yet he'd never touched her, except for that one electrifying instant when she'd been accidentally trapped between him and the refrigerator. She'd anticipated something more when he walked her to her car, and her heart had thundered in her chest. But he'd simply held open the car door, then closed it gently behind her. Only his lazy, lingering gaze had seared her and made her blood run hot.

That heated examination was enough to get the message across with provocative clarity. Nick had more in mind for the two of them. He was only biding his time. The thought scared the daylights out of her. She'd been so sure she had built an impenetrable wall around her emotions, but in Nick's presence that wall was tumbling down. She didn't know quite how she'd ever build it up again.

On Friday she sat on her front porch rocking until long past midnight. Usually listening to the silence and counting the stars scattered across the velvet blanket of darkness soothed her. Every night since she'd come to River Glen, the flower-scented breeze had caressed her so gently that her muscles relaxed and she felt tension ease away. But tonight there was no magic. Cars filled with rowdy teenagers split the silence and clouds covered the stars. The humid night air was as still as death and, in her distraught, churning state of mind, just as ominous.

As a result, she was as nervous and tense when she went in to bed as she had been when she'd first settled into the rocker seeking comfort and an escape from her troubling thoughts. She tried reading, but the words swam before her exhausted eyes. When she turned out the light, she lay in the darkness, staring at the ceiling, first counting sheep, then going over the titles of her favorite books, then counting sheep again.

Although she waged an intense battle to keep the prospect of tomorrow's date out of her mind, it was always there, lurking about the fringes of her thoughts.

It's only one evening, she reminded herself. *Tony will be there. So will half the town, for that matter.*

But even one evening in the company of a man with a surprising power to unnerve her was too much. It loomed before her as an endless ordeal to be gotten through, even though it would drain whatever supreme courage she could still muster from her worn-down defenses. Nick was constantly at the center of her thoughts, and in these thoughts his casual touches branded her in a way that awed and frightened her at the same time.

In reality, he was doing nothing but flirting with her. But how long would it be before those touches became intense, demanding? How long before the pressure would start and the torment would curl inside her like a vicious serpent waiting to strike?

Finally exhaustion claimed her and she fell into a restless, uneasy slumber. Considering her state of mind, it wasn't surprising that she awoke in the middle of the night screaming, her throat hoarse, her whole body trembling and covered with sweat. She sat up in bed shaking, clutching the covers around her, staring blindly into the darkness for the threat that had seemed so real, so familiar. At last, still shivering but convinced it had been only a dream, she reached for the light by her bed to banish the last of the shadows. Her hand was shaking and tears streamed down her face unchecked.

Oh, God, please, when will it end? When will I be free of the memories?

Tonight was the first time in months the nightmare had returned. In her relief, she had even deluded herself that her bad dreams were a thing of the past, that they'd been left behind in a Manhattan skyscraper. She should have known that horror didn't die so easily. Perhaps it was simply because for the first time in months, she had failed to leave a night-light burning, something to keep away the ghosts that haunted her. She vowed never to make that mistake again.

It was hours before she slept again and noon before she woke. Six hours before Nick and Tony were due. Six hours to be gotten through with nerves stretched taut, her mind restless. More than once she reached for the phone to call Nick and cancel, but each time she hung it back up, labeling herself a coward.

It was her first date since Sam, and first times were always the hardest. After tonight, she hoped the jitters would go away, although with Nick Verone, it was quite possible—likely, in fact—that they'd only become worse.

"I can't do it," she muttered at last. "I can't go, if I'm going to jump like a frightened, inexperienced schoolgirl every time the man gets within an inch of me."

This time when she picked up the phone, her hand was steady, her determination intact. The resonant sound of Nick's voice seemed to set off distantly remembered echoes along her spine, but she managed to sound calm and relatively sure of herself when she greeted him.

"Nick, there's a problem." She hesitated, then

hurried on. "I really don't think I'll be able to go with you tonight after all."

"Why?"

"I'm not feeling very well." That, at least, was no lie, but she discovered she was holding her breath as she awaited his reply.

"I'm sorry," he said, and she could hear the genuine regret, the stirring of compassion. He didn't for a single instant suspect her of lying. "Is it the flu? Do you need something from the pharmacy? I could run by the grocery store and pick up some soup or something if you need it."

His unquestioning concern immediately filled her with shame. She swallowed the guilty lump in her throat. "No, it's not the flu," she admitted, closing her eyes so she wouldn't have to look at herself in the mirror over the phone table. "I just had a bad night last night. I didn't get much sleep."

"Is that all?" Nick's relief was evident. "Then take a quick nap. It's only five o'clock now. I'll give you an extra half hour. We won't pick you up until six-thirty. We'll still have plenty of time."

"No, really." She rushed through the words. "I won't be very good company. I appreciate your asking. Maybe another time."

"Now you listen to me," he said, his voice dropping to its sexiest pitch, sliding over her persuasively. "This won't be a late night. I promise. Getting out will probably make you feel better. You'll forget whatever was on your mind, meet some new people, and tonight you'll catch up on your sleep."

Dana could almost envision him nodding his head decisively as he added, "No doubt about it. This is exactly what you need. I'm not taking no for an answer."

"But, Nick—"

"No buts. You're coming with us. If you're not ready when we get there, we'll wait. And what about Tony?" he continued. "You don't want to disappoint him, do you?"

Dana felt the pressure build, but oddly she was almost relieved that Nick wasn't listening to her ridiculous excuses. She had blown this single date out of proportion. Nick was right about her getting out and meeting new people. Maybe it would be the best thing for her to do. Besides, he wasn't about to let up now that he had her on the ropes. She sighed and conceded defeat. "You really don't care what kind of sneaky, rotten tactics you use, do you?"

Nick merely chuckled at her grumbling. "Well, he would be disappointed, wouldn't he? That's the unvarnished truth. I was just trying to point that out to you before you made a dreadful mistake that would make you feel guilty for the rest of your life."

"Precisely. You knew it would work, unless I was on my deathbed, right?"

She could practically visualize Nick's satisfied grin. "It was worth a shot," he agreed. "Did it work?"

"It worked. Make it six-thirty. The idea of a nap sounds wonderful."

"See you then," he said cheerfully. "Sleep well."

"Sleep well," she mimicked when she'd replaced the receiver. Blast the man! The only way she'd sleep now would be to get this evening over with. So instead of lying down, she went to the tomato garden and furiously uprooted every weed she could spot. If she was going to have a temper tantrum, it might as well serve a useful purpose. The tantrum felt good, even if it was misdirected. She could just imagine what the townsfolk would say if she pulled the hairs from Nick Verone's overconfident head just as enthusiastically.

An hour later, after a soothing bubble bath, she dressed with unusual care, wanting to find exactly the right look for her first social appearance in River Glen. The fact that she was making it on the arm of the town's most eligible bachelor should have given her self-confidence. Instead, it made her quake.

Barbecue and bingo hardly called for a silk dress, but jeans were much too casual. She finally settled for a pale blue sleeveless cotton dress that bared the slightly golden tan of her arms but not much else. Its full skirt swirled about her legs. She wore low-heeled sandals, though she had a feeling three-inch heels might improve her confidence. Then she thought of all the times she'd dressed regally in New York and realized the clothes had made no difference at all.

This time she heard Nick's car drive up before she saw him. She'd been pacing from room to room, refusing to sit out on the porch, where it might seem she was waiting for him. Nick called through the screen door in back, rather than knocking, and the sound of his low drawl sent a shiver down her spine. Did she feel dread? Anticipation? Did she even know anymore?

When she came to the door his gaze swept over her appreciatively, then returned to linger on her face. A slow smile lit his rugged features, making him even more handsome.

"Yet another personality," he muttered cryptically.

Dana gave him a puzzled glance. "What does that mean?"

"Last Saturday you could have been a farmer, all covered with dirt and sweat."

She wrinkled her nose. "Sounds attractive. I'm surprised you asked me out."

A teasing glint appeared in his tawny eyes. "I knew you'd clean up good. Monday proved it. You could have been working on Wall Street instead of our library in that outfit. The only thing missing was the briefcase."

"And now?"

"I'm not sure. I only wish we were going square dancing, so that skirt could fly up and—"

"Never mind," she interrupted quickly. "I get the idea."

"I hope so," he said so softly it raised goose bumps on her arms. Unfortunately, her reaction was all too visible and Nick was rogue enough to take pleasure in it. He shot a very confident grin her way.

It was going to be a very long evening.

Despite his compliments and light flirting, Nick had noticed something else when Dana greeted him, something he politely didn't mention. The woman was exhausted. That story she'd spun on the phone to try to get out of their date hadn't been as manufactured as it had sounded. Underneath the skillful makeup, her complexion was ashen and there were deep, dark smudges under her eyes. Something was clearly troubling her, but he doubted if she'd bring it up and he had a feeling she wouldn't appreciate it if he did.

At Gracie's, where the tablecloths were plastic and the saltshakers were clogged because of the humidity, huge fans whirred overhead to stir the unseasonably sultry air. As they entered, every head in the place turned curiously to study the three of them with unabashed interest. Dana flinched imperceptibly under the scrutiny, but

Nick caught her discomfort and they hurried straight to a table, rather than lingering to exchange greetings. He told himself there would be time enough for introductions at the fire station.

"So, what's it gonna be, Nick?" Carla Redding asked, stepping up to the table and leaning down just enough to display her ample cleavage.

Nick grinned at her and never once let his gaze wander lower than her round, rosy-cheeked face. "Are you trying to hustle us out of here in a hurry tonight, so you can pick up more tips? We haven't even seen the menu."

Carla straightened up and tugged a pencil out from behind her ear. "Menu hasn't changed in ten years, as you know perfectly well, since you eat here at least twice a week."

"But we have a newcomer with us tonight. This is Dana Brantley, the new librarian. Dana, meet Carla Redding. She owns this place."

"But I thought this was Gracie's," she said, as Nick chuckled at Dana's obvious confusion.

Carla grinned. "It was Gracie's when I bought it ten years ago. Saw no need to change it. Just mixes people up. You need to see a menu, honey?"

"Nick claims you have the best barbecue around, so I suppose I ought to have that."

"Good choice," Nick said. "We'll have four barbecue sandwiches." He glanced at Tony, who seemed to be growing at the rate of an inch a day lately. "Nope. Better make that five. Some coleslaw, french fries and how about some apple pie? Did you do any baking today?"

"I've got one hidden in the back just for you," she said with a wink as she ruffled Tony's hair. Nick glanced over to check Dana's reaction to Carla's determinedly provocative display of affection. He and Carla had gone through school together. There was nothing between them—not now, not ever. But from the look on Dana's face, he doubted she'd believe it.

As soon as Carla had gone back to the kitchen, Dana commented, "Interesting woman."

"She and Dad are old friends," Tony offered innocently.

"I'll bet."

Nick chuckled. "Her husband's a friend of mine, too. Jack has the size and temperament of a tanker. Carla just loves to flirt outrageously with all her male customers. She says it keeps Jack on his toes."

She grinned back. "I don't doubt it for a minute. She's very convincing."

Nick feigned astonishment and leaned over to whisper in her ear, "Don't tell me you were jealous?"

"Of course not," she denied heatedly.

But from that moment on, to Nick's dismay the evening went from bad to worse. Rather than the natural, somewhat aggrieved banter he'd come to expect, Dana was making an effort to be polite and pleasant. Her laughter was strained and all too often her attention seemed to wander to a place where Nick couldn't follow. Only with Tony was she completely at ease. A lesser man's ego might have been shattered, but Dana's behavior merely perplexed Nick.

Even in the small, friendly crowd at bingo, Dana seemed alienated and nervous, as though torn between wanting to make a good impression and a desire to retreat. Somehow he knew she suffered from more than shyness, but he couldn't imagine what the problem was.

When he could stand the awkwardness no longer, he suggested they take a walk. Dana glanced up from her bingo card in surprise. They were in the middle of a game and she had four of five spaces for a diagonal win.

"Now?" she said.

"Sure. I need some air." He saw her gaze go immediately to Tony, so he said, "You'll be okay here for a few minutes, won't you, son?"

"Sure, Dad. I'll play your cards for you." He looked as though he could hardly wait to get a shot at Dana's.

With obvious reluctance Dana got to her feet and followed him outside. There was the clean scent of rain in the air. Thunder rumbled ominously in the distance.

"Seems like there's a storm brewing," he said,

as they strolled side by side until the sounds from the fire station became a distant murmur.

"It is April, after all," she replied.

The inconsequential conversation suddenly grated across his nerves. Nick was a direct man. Too direct for politics, some said. He had a feeling that's what they'd be saying if they could see him now, but he couldn't keep his thoughts to himself another second.

"What's troubling you, Dana? You've been jumpy as a cat on a hot tin roof all night."

"Sorry."

He felt an unfamiliar urge to shake her until the truth rattled loose. In fact, he reached for her shoulders but restrained himself at the last instant, stunned by what he'd been about to do. No woman had ever driven him to such conflicting feelings of helplessness and rage before. "Dammit, I don't want you to apologize. I want to help. Did I do something to upset you?"

Astonishment registered in her brown eyes before she could conceal it. "Why would you think that?"

"I don't know. Maybe it's just the way you went all silent after I teased you about being jealous back at Gracie's. You haven't said more than two words at a time since then except to Tony."

"Jealousy is a very negative emotion," she responded slowly, her expression distant again. "It's not something I like to joke about."

"I take it you've had some experience."

She nodded, but it was clear no personal confidences would be forthcoming. She had that closed look in her eyes, and it tore at him to see anyone hurting and seemingly so alone. The depth of his protectiveness startled him. It hinted of the sweet and abiding passion he'd felt only once before, with Ginny, whom he'd known all his life and who had hidden a gentle heart behind a determinedly tough tomboy facade. She'd accepted his protection only at the end, when cancer had riddled her body with pain.

Somehow he knew that Dana would be just as unwilling to permit him to take up her battles. Despite her vulnerability she had a resilience that he admired. He had been intrigued by her even before they'd met, because of her kindness to Tony. It had been uncalculated giving, unlike so many attempts he'd seen by single women to reach him through his son. Tony had sung her praises for days before Nick decided to meet her for himself. Her leaky roof had been no more than an excuse at first. Now he wondered if it might be the only link she would permit.

Suddenly Nick realized that Dana was shivering. He hadn't noticed that the wind had picked up and that the air had cooled considerably as the storm blew in. He also hadn't realized just how far they'd walked while he tried to sort out his thoughts.

"You're cold," he said. "Let's go back."

"Would you mind terribly if we just got Tony and left?"

Nick sighed. "I hope it's not because I've stuck my foot in my mouth again."

"No. It's just that it's getting late and I really am tired."

Nick studied her face closely. He wanted to trace the shadows under her eyes, run his fingers along the delicate curve of her jaw, but he held back from that as cautiously as he'd kept himself from that more violent urge.

"Fine," he said eventually. "I'll get Tony."

The storm began with a lashing fury as he walked Dana back to the car. Nick took her hand and they broke into a run, hurrying to the relative safety of a darkened doorway. Both of them were soaked through, and as they huddled side by side, Nick's gaze fell on the way Dana's dress clung to her breasts. The peaks had hardened in the chilly air and jutted against the damp fabric. Tension coiled inside him. Dana shivered again and before he had a chance to consider what he was doing, he drew her into his arms.

She went absolutely rigid in his embrace. "Nick." His name came out as a choked entreaty.

"Shh. It's okay," he murmured, wondering how anything that felt so right to him could possibly scare her so. And he didn't doubt that she was afraid. He felt it in her frozen stance, saw the startled nervousness that had leaped into her eyes at his touch. "I just want to keep you warm until we can make a break for the car."

"I—I'll b-b-be fine."

"Your teeth are chattering."

"N-n-no, they're n-not," she said, defiant to the end. She struggled against him.

"Dana." This time his voice was thick with emotion and an unspoken plea.

Her gaze shot up and clashed with his. Then she held herself perfectly still, and he felt her slowly begin to relax in his arms.

The rain pounded down harder than ever, creating a gray, wet sheet that secluded them from the rest of the world. Nick could have stayed like that forever. Holding Dana in his arms felt exactly as he'd imagined it would. Her body fit his perfectly, the soft contours molding themselves to the hard planes of his own overheated flesh. He felt the sharp stirring in his loins again and wondered if he could fight it by concentrating on the distant sounds of laughter and shouts of victory drifting from the fire station down the block.

"Nick?" Her tentative voice whispered down his spine like the fingers of an expert masseuse.

"Yes."

"I have to get home." The words held an odd urgency. At his puzzled expression, she added, "The roof."

"The roof," he repeated blankly, still lost in the sensations that were rippling through him.

"I put the pots and pans away. The whole place will be flooded if this keeps up."

"Right. The roof." Reluctantly, he released her. He looked into the velvet brown of her eyes and saw that miraculously the panic had fled, but he wasn't sure how to describe the complexity of the emotion that had replaced it. Surprise, dismay, acceptance. Any of those or maybe all of them. Relief and hope flooded through him.

"You wait here. I'll go back for Tony and the car."

"I'm already drenched. I can come with you."

With her words, his eyes were drawn back to the swell of her breast, unmistakably detailed by her clinging dress. He held out his hand, and after an instant's hesitation, she took it.

"Let's run for it," he said, and they took off, her long-legged strides keeping up with his intentionally shortened paces. Rain pelted them with the force of hailstones, but they splashed through the puddles with all the abandon of a couple of kids. For the first time all night Dana seemed totally at ease.

When they reached the car, she moaned softly. "Your upholstery."

"Will survive," he said. "Now get in there. I think I have a blanket in the trunk. I'll get it for you."

He found an old sandy beach blanket and shook it out before draping it around her shaking shoulders.

"Is that better?"

"Much, thanks." She smiled up at him with the first unguarded expression he'd seen on her face all night. It had been worth the wait and he was tempted to stay and bask in its warmth.

Instead, he nodded. "Good. I'll be back in a minute with Tony."

He walked into the fire station and scanned the room for his son. Water ran down his face in rivulets and squished from his shoes. Puddles formed where he stood.

Betsy Markham sashayed up and gave him a sweet, innocent smile. "Been for a walk?"

"Something like that."

"And here I always thought you have sense enough to come in out of the rain, Nicholas. Must be a pretty girl involved."

"Could be, Betsy."

Suddenly her expression turned serious and she wagged a finger under his nose. "You see to it that gal doesn't get pneumonia, Nick Verone, or I'll have your hide."

A chuckle rumbled up through his chest. He grabbed Betsy by the shoulders and planted a kiss on her cheek. She smelled of talcum powder and lily of the valley, just as his mother always had. His hands left wet marks on her shoulders, but she gave him a wink as she went back to her place beside her husband. Nick watched as the intent expression on Harry's face changed to delight when he looked up and saw Betsy. He saw Harry's arm slip affectionately around her waist for a quick squeeze before his attention went back to the game.

"Hey, Dad, what happened to you?" Tony regarded his father with astonishment. "You're dripping all over everything."

"In case you haven't noticed, it's raining outside. Dana and I got caught in it. We've got to get her home."

"Aw, Dad, come on. It's early. Why don't I wait here? You can come back for me." He cast an all-too-knowing look up at his father. "You and Ms. Brantley probably want to be alone, anyway, right? I mean that's how you got wet in the first place, trying to be alone with her."

Nick managed a stern expression, though he was fighting laughter. Ignoring Tony's incredibly accurate assessment of his desires with regard to Dana, he said firmly, "You'll come with us now."

Tony knew that no-nonsense tone of voice. He shrugged and headed for the door without another protest. Nick stared after his son and wondered what perversity of his own nature had made him insist that Tony come with him.

"It's for the best," he muttered under his breath

and he knew it was true. He wanted Dana Brantley, and without Tony along he might very well ruin things by showing her that. Whatever trust had just been born was still too fragile to be tested by any aggressive moves.

The rain let up as they drove to Dana's place. When he pulled up in front and shut off the engine, she turned to him. "You don't have to walk me in."

"Yes, I do. You could have a foot of water inside."

"I can take care of it."

"I'm sure you can, but why should you, when Tony and I can help?" He was out of the car before she could utter another protest. "Son, you wait here a minute until I check things out. If we need you, I'll yell."

"Right, Dad," Tony said agreeably, though there was a smirk on his face.

Dana was already up the walk and around the side of the house. He caught up with her as she tried to put the key in the door. It was pitch-dark and her hands were shaking. She kept missing the lock. Nick nudged her aside. "Let me."

"I forgot to leave the light on."

"No problem." The door swung open. He reached in and flipped on the kitchen and outdoor lights. "Let's check the damage."

There were pools of water on the floor in at least half a dozen places. "Where's your mop?"

"I'll do it," she insisted obstinately, a scowl on her face. "It's not that bad."

He planted his feet more firmly and glowered down at her. "You are without a doubt the stubbornest woman I have ever met."

Dana glared back at him. "And you're the stubbornest man I've ever met, so where does that leave us?"

"With a wet floor, unless you'll get the mop."

She whirled around and stomped away, returning with the sponge mop and a bucket. He grinned at her. "Thank you."

She perched on the edge of a chair and watched him work, a puzzled expression in her eyes. "I've been perfectly rotten to you all night and you're still hanging around. I don't understand it. Are you afflicted with some sort of damsel-in-distress syndrome?"

"Not that I know of."

"Then it must be a straightforward, macho mentality."

"Maybe I'm just a nice guy. You don't have to be macho to wield a mop."

"Exactly my point. I could have done this."

"Do you have some sort of independence syndrome?" he countered.

"As a matter of fact, I do," she said so softly that his head snapped up and he stared at her. Suddenly he realized that whatever was wrong went far beyond who mopped the floor.

"What happened to you that makes you want to close out people who care about you?"

She appeared disconcerted by the directness of the question. "That's none of your business."

"It is if I'm going to get to know you better."

"Like I said, it's none of your business." She got up and walked back into the kitchen, leaving Nick to mop alone and mull over the conversation. He'd just been granted an important clue to Dana's personality. Now he had only to figure out what it meant.

When he finished, he found Dana sitting at the kitchen table, her chin propped in her hand. She was staring out the door, a faraway expression in her eyes. Nick wanted to pull up a chair right then and finish their talk, but with Tony in the car, he couldn't. He'd already left him out there alone too long.

"I'll come over tomorrow and work on the roof," he announced quietly. Dana looked up at him, and for an instant, a challenge flared in her eyes. Then it died. She nodded, and for some reason Nick considered her acquiescence a major victory. He had the strangest sensation that she'd been unconsciously testing him all evening and that without knowing exactly how, he'd passed.

She stood up and walked him to the door, standing on the top step so that her eyes were even with his.

"Thank you," she said in a low whisper, pitched

to match the night's quiet serenity now that the storm had gone.

"Did you have a good time, really?"

"Of course. It was my first chance to meet so many people. I enjoyed it."

The words were polite, the tone flat. Nick pressed a finger to her lips, wanting to silence the lies. He smiled. "Then maybe next time you'll look a little happier."

Dana flushed in embarrassment. "I'm sorry. I didn't realize . . ." She sighed. "I didn't mean to be rude."

"No, I'm the one who's sorry. I shouldn't have made such a big deal of it. Maybe sometime you'll tell me what really went wrong tonight."

"Nick—"

"Shh." He rubbed his finger across the soft flesh of her lips. "Don't deny it. Please."

Her eyes brimmed with tears, and she swiped at them with the same angry motion as a child who shows weakness when he craves bravery. She would have turned away to hide the raw emotion in her eyes, but Nick caught her chin and held her face steady before him.

"You're so beautiful, Dana Brantley. Inside and out. How could any woman as lovely as you have so much to be sad about?"

He caught a tiny flicker of something in her eyes—surprise, perhaps, that he'd guessed at the sadness that hid under her cool demeanor and quiet laughter. She licked her lips nervously and he couldn't take his eyes from the ripe moistness.

But when he leaned forward to kiss her, his heart pounding and his pulse racing, she pulled away, turning her face aside. Intuitively he knew it wasn't a coy reaction. There had been a real panic in her eyes. Again. He felt a hurt, one he imagined was every bit as great as hers, building up inside. God, he'd give anything to make things better for her, to make those smiles come more frequently, to hear the laughter without the restraint.

But Nick hadn't made a success of himself in business without knowing when to back away, when to let a deal simmer until the other person was just as hungry for a resolution. In time Dana would acknowledge that her hunger for him ran just as deep, was just as powerful as his was for her.

He brushed away a lone tear as it glistened on her cheek. "Good night, pretty lady. I'll see you in the morning."

He had nearly turned the corner of the house before he heard her faint response carried by the breeze.

"Goodbye, Nick."

There was a finality in her voice that sent a shiver down his spine. It also fueled his determination. This would not be an ending for them. It was just the beginning.

Chapter 4

"Don't you like my dad?" Tony asked Dana with all the disconcerting candor of an irrepressible ten-year-old. She came very close to choking on the glazed doughnut they'd just shared as they sat on her back step.

At least he'd waited until they were alone to start his cross-examination. Nick was on the roof, stripping off the old shingles. It was Sunday morning, and Tony and Nick had been on her doorstep practically at dawn, a bag of fresh doughnuts and a huge, intimidating toolbox in hand. Her eyes had met Nick's, then darted away as an unexpected thrill had coursed through her. She tried to recapture that sensation, so she could assess it rationally, but Tony was staring at her, waiting for her answer.

"He's very nice," Dana equivocated. Tony looked disappointed by the lukewarm praise.

Damn it all, the man was more than nice, she acknowledged to herself, even though she absolutely refused to acknowledge it aloud. Last night she had been rude and withdrawn without fully understanding why, but Nick had shown only compassion in return. She had sensed his struggle to understand behavior

75

that must have seemed decidedly odd to him.

No doubt most women were eager for an involvement with one of the most powerful, eligible men in River Glen. At some other time in her life, she might have been one of them, but now that was impossible. She had nothing but trouble to bring to a relationship. And she knew as well as anyone that involvement always began with something as sweet and innocent as a kiss.

She'd given marriage a chance. Sam Brantley had been handsome, charming and brilliant—a real catch, as Betsy would say. There had been a classic explosion of chemistry the night they met, followed by a storybook courtship, then a lavish wedding and an idyllic honeymoon.

Dana had been twenty-three, only months away from receiving her master's degree, but she had given up school willingly to help Sam meet the social obligations of a young lawyer on the rise in a prestigious New York firm. They were the perfect couple, living in the best East Side condo, spending much of their spare time with the right friends at gala events for the most socially acceptable charities.

It had been slightly less than a year before the reality set in, before the pressures of keeping up began to take their toll. By their first anniversary, their marriage was already in trouble. It took much longer to end it.

She closed her eyes against the rest of the

memories, the months of torment that had turned into years. It was over now. The past couldn't hurt her anymore unless she allowed it. And she wouldn't. She had put it behind her with a vow it would stay locked away forever.

"Are you okay?" Tony's brow was furrowed by a worried frown. "You look all funny."

"I'm just fine," she said as cheerfully as she could manage.

Tony looked doubtful but then plunged on with determination. "Then explain about my dad. If you think he's nice, how come you didn't kiss him last night? I know he wanted you to."

Dana was torn between indignation and laughter. "Tony Verone, were you spying on us?"

"I wasn't spying," he denied, his cheeks reddening with embarrassment. "Not the way you mean. Dad was gone a long time. I got tired of waiting in the car by myself. I decided to come check on him. That's all. That's not really spying."

"Your father would tan your hide if he knew what you'd done."

"No, he wouldn't," Tony said with absolute confidence. "He never spanks me. He says people should be able to talk out their differences, even kids and parents."

It sounded as though he were quoting an oft-repeated conversation. The significance of Nick's philosophy of discipline registered in a corner of Dana's mind and she stored it away. She regarded Tony closely. "In that case, you'd be getting quite a lecture, wouldn't you?"

Tony met her gaze with a defiant challenge in his eyes, then hung his head guiltily. "Probably."

"Then I've made my point."

"Yeah. I guess."

"Now that that's settled, why don't you go inside and do your book report?"

"Okay," he said a little too agreeably, getting up from the step and heading inside. He opened the screen door, then gazed back at her inquisitively. "You're not really mad, are you?"

Dana smiled. "No, I'm not really mad."

Tony nodded in satisfaction. "So, are you going to kiss him next time?"

"Tony!"

"Yes, ma'am," he said politely, but there was an impertinent glint in his eyes that reminded her very much of his father.

Dana had to turn her face away to hide her smile until Tony had gone into the house. The kid was something else. Would she kiss his father next time? What a question!

Well, will you? a voice inside her head nagged.

"No, dammit," she said aloud, then glanced around quickly to make sure that no one had caught her talking to herself.

"Who are you talking to down there?" a voice inquired from above her head.

"I was just asking if you wanted something to drink," she improvised hurriedly.

"Oh, is *that* what you said?" Nick's voice was filled with amusement.

Maybe she should have a talk with him about eavesdropping. Then again, maybe there had been all too much talk around here this morning as it was.

She stepped out into the yard, then shielded her eyes from the sun as she scowled up at the roof. "Well, do you want something or not?"

He came to the edge, moving gingerly around the weak spots. Dana gazed at him and her breath caught in her throat. He'd stripped off his shirt as he worked and his tanned, well-muscled shoulders were glistening with sweat. Dark hairs swirled in a damp mass on his broad chest and narrowed provocatively down to the waistband of his jeans.

"I'd love some lemonade," he said.

"I don't think I have any," she murmured in a distracted tone, fighting the surprisingly strong urge to climb straight up to the roof so she could run her fingers over his bare flesh. She hadn't felt this powerful, aching need to touch and be touched in a very long time.

"I thought everybody had lemonade."

"What?" she said blankly, forcing her eyes back to his. That was a mistake, too, because there was a very knowing gleam in their hazel depths.

"I said I thought everybody had lemonade," he repeated tolerantly.

Dana clenched her fists, now fighting a desire not just to touch but to strangle the man. "Not me. Your choices are juice, iced tea, diet soda or water."

"But I have a yen for . . ." His eyes roamed over her boldly before he added with slow deliberation, "Lemonade."

"Nick," she snapped impatiently.

He chuckled at her obvious discomfort, apparently enjoying the heightened color in her cheeks. "Send Tony to the store. He can run up there and back in fifteen minutes."

"He's inside, doing his homework. If you can't live without lemonade, I'll go."

"Tony!" he called as though she'd never spoken.

The back door crashed open all too quickly and Dana got the oddest sensation that Tony had been waiting just inside. His refusal to meet her gaze as he stepped out to look up at his father virtually confirmed it.

"What do you need, Dad?"

"How about running to the store for me?" Nick climbed down the ladder, dug in his pocket and gave Tony some money and a list of provisions long enough to stock a refrigerator for a month.

When he'd gone, Dana glowered at Nick. "Why did you do that? I could have gone."

"But then we wouldn't have had a few minutes alone." He stepped toward her. Dana held her ground, but her pulse began to race.

"A few minutes? It'll take him the better part of an hour to get all those things. Are you planning to feed an entire army?"

"Just us. I'm very hungry," he retorted, drawing the words out to an insinuating suggestiveness. "And I want to know, just as much as Tony does, why you didn't kiss me."

Dana swallowed nervously. "I don't kiss men I don't know well." She sounded extraordinarily self-righteous and absurdly Victorian, even to her own ears.

"Who's fault is it we don't know each other better? I'm trying to change that." He took another step toward her. This time she backed up instinctively.

"Why did you do that?" he asked, and she could see he was more curious than angry.

"Do what?"

"Move away from me." A frown knit his brow. "Do I frighten you?"

"Of course not."

"Liar," he accused gently. "I do, don't I?"

"Don't be absurd."

He stood perfectly still, like a hunter waiting for his prey to be disarmed and drawn into his range. "Then let me kiss you, Dana."

His voice was a quiet plea that set off a violent

trembling inside her. He wooed her with that voice.

"Dana, I'm not going to hurt you. Not ever."

There was so much tenderness in his voice. It touched a place deep inside her and filled her with unexpected warmth. Her eyes widened in anticipation, but he didn't move.

Finally, he sighed. "Someday, I hope you'll believe me."

His hand trembling, he brushed his knuckles gently along her cheek, then started back up the ladder. After he'd turned away, her hand went to her cheek and stayed there. With unwilling fascination, she watched the bunching of his muscles as Nick reached over his head to pull himself onto the roof. She heard the hammering begin again, and then, finally, she went inside, her knees as weak as if she'd just escaped from some terrible danger.

And she had. Nick Verone was getting to her. She could deny it all she liked. She could hold him at arm's length, but she knew perfectly well what was happening between them, and for the first time she began to sense the inevitability of it. She almost regretted not letting Nick kiss her now, not getting the agony of anticipation over with.

His backing off, however, both puzzled and pleased her. She had no doubt that Nick desired her. She'd seen the rise of heat in his eyes. But his willingness to wait told her quite a lot about his character and his patience. If they were ever to have a chance, he needed to have both.

To Dana it was soon apparent that Nick had more character than patience. Oblivious to her determination to avoid a relationship—or simply choosing to ignore her wishes, which was more likely—Nick Verone persisted in his pursuit throughout the following week. She had to give him credit. He was subtle and wily and he wasn't one bit above using Tony as his intermediary. He'd sensed that Tony was her weakness, that she would no more see the boy hurt than he would. It was Tony, as often as not, who suggested a drive in the country after the library doors were closed for the day. Or the fishing after Nick had spent an hour or two working on the roof. Or the twilight picnics on the beach.

With Tony along, she began to relax. By the end of the week she found that she was enjoying herself, smiling more frequently, laughing more freely, no longer frightened by shadows. She was actually disappointed when neither of them suggested an outing for the weekend.

On Saturday morning, feeling thoroughly disgruntled and furious because she felt that way, she pulled on her dirt-streaked gardening shorts and tied her sleeveless shirt just under her breasts. As soon as she'd finished her coffee, she went outside to tackle the thick tangle of weeds in the bed of tiger lilies. Sitting on the still damp grass, she yanked and grumbled.

"So, you don't have plans for the weekend. Big deal. You're the one who doesn't want to get involved."

The bright tiger lilies trembled in the stiff breeze coming off the river, but whatever opinion they might have had, they kept to themselves.

"Not talking, huh? That's okay. I can keep myself company." Had it been only a week ago that she'd craved being alone? Had it taken so little time for Nick to overcome her caution and become a welcome part of her life? "You made a humdinger of a mistake last time, Dana Brantley. Don't do it again."

"Talking to yourself again?" Nick inquired softly.

Dana's head snapped around so quickly she almost got whiplash. "Where do you have your car's engine tuned? Your mechanic must be a genius. I didn't even hear you drive up."

"No car," he said, pointing to the very obvious bike he was holding upright by its handlebars. His gaze traveled slowly over her, lingering on the expanse of golden skin between her blouse and shorts. "Nice outfit."

"You commented on it before. I believe you referred to it as my farmer look."

"I take it back. You're prettier than any farmer I ever saw, though I know a couple of farmers' wives who'd give you a run for your money."

"I'll just bet you do."

Nick pulled the bike onto the grass and laid it on its side, then headed for the house. Dana stared after him in exasperation. He was doing it again, just dropping in and taking over as though he belonged. One of these days they were going to have a very noisy confrontation about his behavior.

"Where are you going?" she inquired testily.

"To get some coffee. You have some made, don't you?"

"Of course, but . . ."

He was out of sight before she could finish her protest. "Back in a minute," he called over his shoulder.

Sparks flashed in her eyes, but just as she was about to stand up and go storming in the house after him, he shouted out, "Hey, do you want any?"

"Nice of you to ask," she grumbled under her breath. She peered in the direction of the kitchen and called back, "No."

She yanked a few more weeds out of the ground and tossed them aside with more force than was necessary. A colorful variety of names for the man now in her kitchen paraded through her mind. "Why don't you speak up and tell him he's driving you crazy?" she muttered aloud.

But she knew she wouldn't. She couldn't face

the potential explosiveness of angry threats, the tension that made your heart pound, even the mild stomach-churning sensation of seeing control slip away.

"How long are you planning to be at that?" Nick suddenly inquired, hunkering down beside her.

Dana jumped a good three inches off the ground. "Dammit, Nick. Stop sneaking up on me."

"Sorry." He didn't look one bit sorry. "What's on your agenda for the day?"

"I don't have an agenda." She paused thoughtfully. "Do you know this is practically the first time in my life I can say that? First it was ballet lessons, then gymnastics, then piano. By the time I got to high school, it was cheerleading, half a dozen clubs and tennis lessons. College was more of the same and my marriage was a merry-go-round of luncheons and dinner parties and bridge. I don't think I ever had ten unscheduled minutes until I moved here."

"Good, then you can come with me."

Dana regarded him warily. "Where?"

"I thought we might go for a long bike ride."

"Don't you have things to do?"

"Nothing that appeals to me more than spending the day with you."

"Where's Tony?"

"He's at a friend's." He draped his arm casually over her shoulders and squeezed. "It's just you and me, kid."

The phrase reverberated through her head and set off warning signals, but that was nothing compared to the skyrockets set off by his touch. She started to look at Nick but realized he was much too close and turned away. She'd have been staring straight at his lips and she had a feeling she wouldn't be able to hide her fascination with them. Ever since she'd avoided his kiss after bingo and again on Sunday, she'd been wondering what his lips would have felt like, imagined them brushing lightly across her mouth or kissing the sensitive spot on her neck, just below her ear.

"I don't have a bike."

"No problem. You can borrow Tony's."

"I haven't ridden in years."

"It's something you never forget."

"But my legs are in terrible condition." Nick's dubious expression as his eyes traveled the length of said legs almost made her laugh, but she rushed on. "I wouldn't make it around the block."

"We'll only ride until you get tired."

"If we ride until I can't go any farther, how will we get back?"

"Hopefully you'll have the good sense to complain in front of some nice, air-conditioned restaurant so we can have lunch while you recuperate."

"We may need to have dinner and breakfast before that happens."

"I can live with that," he said with a dangerously

wicked sparkle in his eyes. "Just be sure to collapse in front of an inn."

Dana laughed, suddenly feeling a carefree, what-the-hell sensation ripple pleasantly through her. It had been a long time since she'd done anything on the spur of the moment. "I give up. You have an answer for everything, don't you?"

"I am a very determined man," he replied so solemnly that her heart raced. She avoided his clear-eyed, direct gaze as she got to her feet. "Let me take these weeds to the garbage and change. Then I'll be all set."

"I'll take the weeds. You go and get dressed."

A half hour later, after a wobbly start on Dana's part, they were on the road. Once she got the hang of riding again, it felt terrific. The spring sun was warm on her shoulders, the breeze cool on her face.

"This is wonderful," she called out to Nick, who was riding ahead of her past a huge brown field that was dotted with corn seedlings. He dropped back to ride beside her.

"Aren't you glad I didn't pay any attention to your excuses again?"

"Very."

"Can I ask you something?"

"Of course."

"Why do you need the excuses in the first place? Do you really want me to back off?"

Dana's heart thudded slowly in her chest. She

met Nick's curious gaze and her pedaling faltered. She caught herself just before the bike went out of control. Staring straight ahead, she finally said, "It probably would be for the best."

"Best for whom? Not for me. I've enjoyed being with you the past few days. It's been a long time since I felt this way."

"What way?"

He seemed to be searching for words. The ones he found were eloquent. "As though my life was filled with possibilities again. When Ginny died, I didn't think I'd ever care for another woman. We'd had a lifetime together and that was important to me. We'd played together, tended to each other's cuts and bruises, gone to school together. We'd grown up together. There were no secrets, no surprises. We were blessed with love and understanding and we were blessed with Tony."

Dana heard the sorrow behind Nick's words, but she also heard the joy. For the first time in her life she was struck by an envy so sharp it rocked her. She wanted to share somehow in that enviable life Nick had led.

"Tell me about Ginny," she said, a catch in her voice.

Nick studied her closely. "Are you sure you want to hear about her?"

"Absolutely. I want to know what she was like, what you loved about her."

He nodded. "Okay, but let's get to a stopping place first."

A few hundred feet farther down the road, he pulled into the gravel parking lot in front of a small country store and gas station.

"I'll get us some soft drinks and a couple of sandwiches, okay?"

"Fine."

Dana propped her bike against the weathered side of the store and stared around her at the recently planted fields that were just beginning to turn green. She felt the same sense of peace and continuity she'd experienced when she'd discovered River Glen. She wanted to draw that feeling inside, to capture it and put her heart at rest. The air was heavy with the rich scent of the fields, the sun was hot on her skin, and she felt more contented than she had in years.

When Nick came out a few minutes later, she realized he was becoming a part of her contentment. There were no jarring notes with Nick, only an easygoing calm that fit well with the surroundings. If only that calm were real, she might dare to hope again.

"There's a place up ahead where we can sit under the trees for a while," he said, and led the way.

When they were settled on the cool grass, he opened the bag and handed her a drink, then held out the sandwiches. "Ham and cheese or tuna?"

"Ham and cheese," she said instantly.

Nick made a face. "I should have known."

"Is that what you wanted? Take it. I like tuna just as well."

"No you don't or you would have asked for it. Take the ham and cheese."

"We'll split them." She was proud of her ingenuity until she caught the expression in Nick's eyes. "What?"

"Why do you do that? Why do you go to such lengths to avoid an argument?"

Dana stared down at the ground. "I wasn't aware that's what I was doing. I just thought it would be nicer if we shared."

He shook his head. "It's more than that. There have been times in the past week when I know you've been furious with me. . . ." He waved aside her instinctive denial. "No. It's true. But you've never once done more than snap a little. Sometimes I want to do outrageous things, just to see how you'll react."

"I don't see much point in arguing."

"Not even when you have a valid difference of opinion?"

"It depends on how important it is. If it's something that doesn't matter, like the sandwiches, it's easier to give in."

"And that's all it is?"

"What else could it be?" she said, retreating behind her shuttered expression again.

Nick felt like pounding the earth or snatching the damn tuna sandwich out of her hands. He wanted, just once, to see her reach her limits and say exactly what she thought, instead of tiptoeing around anything that wasn't pleasant.

It was Dana who broke the silence. "Do you realize how absurd we sound? We're sitting here fighting because I don't like to argue."

"I don't want to fight with you, Dana. I just want to be sure you're not afraid to say what you mean with me. You're entitled to your opinion, even when we disagree. That's what makes life interesting. If we agreed on every single thing, we'd be bored to tears in no time."

"You may be sorry you said that."

"Oh?"

"Once I get started, I might give you a very rough time."

"I'll survive."

Dana nodded. "Okay, Mr. Verone, from now on, you'll only hear the unvarnished truth from me. Now, you were going to tell me about Ginny."

"So I was."

Nick leaned back against the tree and let his mind drift back over the years of his marriage, over the entire lifetime he'd shared with Ginny. With three years of perspective, he could finally recall the good times, rather than dwell on those last painful months.

"She was someone very special," he said at last.

A faint smile lit his face. "I remember once when we were maybe six or seven. My mom had bought strawberries to make strawberry short-cake for a big family dinner. Ginny was crazy about strawberries and she saw them sitting on the kitchen table and she couldn't resist. She climbed up on a chair and started eating. I kept begging her to get down, but she wouldn't. She just sat there with bright red juice all over her face and hands, stuffing them in.

"Then my mom came in. Oh, boy, was there hell to pay. Ginny just listened to her, then said, bold as you please, 'Nick dared me to.' "

Dana grinned. "I suppose you're the one who got punished."

"I spent the rest of the day in my room." He chuckled. "But it wasn't so bad. Ginny climbed a tree right outside the window and talked to me till suppertime."

"Did you always know you wanted to marry her?"

Nick grew thoughtful. "I think I did. I know there was never anyone else. I never met another woman who had her spirit, who reached out and grabbed the day and held on to it until she'd lived every single moment. Yet, for all that fire, she was also very gentle and caring."

He glanced up and met Dana's eyes, caught the tears shimmering in them. "In so many ways, you remind me of her."

Dana was shaking her head. "No, you're wrong. I'm not like that at all."

"I think you are. I see it in everything you do."

"But I don't take risks. You said it yourself. I just drift along, trying to keep things on an even keel."

He regarded her perceptively. "But I don't think you were always like that."

Dana closed her eyes as if to ward off some pain inflicted by his words. He reached over and touched her cheek, his callused thumb following the line of her jaw.

"Dana," he said softly.

Her eyes opened and a tear slid along her cheek.

"That is the woman I see when I look at you."

"You're wrong," she protested. "I wish I were like that, but I'm not."

"Then use my eyes as your mirror," he said gently. "See yourself as I do."

He knelt on the ground beside her, and this time when he lowered his head to kiss her she didn't pull away. Her lips trembled beneath his, then parted on a sigh. She tasted of sunshine and tears, a blend as intoxicating as champagne. He felt her restraint in the rigid way she held her body, in the stiffness of her shoulders, but her mouth was his, and for now, it was enough.

Chapter 5

Over the next few days, Nick thought about very little besides that kiss. It had brought him an incredible depth of satisfaction. He recalled in heart-stopping detail the velvet touch of Dana's lips against his, the moist fire of her tongue, the sweetness of her breath. The memory of each second stirred a joy and longing in him that went far beyond the physical implications of a single kiss.

Each time he replayed the scene in his mind it sent fire raging through his blood. He felt like an adolescent. His body responded to provocative images as easily as it had to the reality. Far more important, however, that kiss had told him that Dana was beginning to trust him. He was wise enough to see that earning Dana's trust in full would be no easy task.

As anxious as any lover—and astonished by the sudden return of the special and rare tug of deep emotion—he could hardly wait to see her when he returned from a four-day business trip. It was Thursday, one of the two nights the library stayed open until nine. He saw the lights burning in the windows when he drove into town. With Tony safely with Ginny's parents there was no reason he couldn't stop. No one expected him until tomorrow, but he'd been too impatient to see Dana to stay away another night.

He found her putting books back on the shelves. She didn't see him as he stood at the end of the aisle, watching as she lifted her arms and stood on tiptoe to reach the top shelf. Her hair had been swept up on top of her head in a knot, but curling tendrils had escaped and curved along her cheeks and down the nape of her neck. The little makeup she normally wore had worn away, leaving her lips a natural pink and her cheeks flushed from the effort of lifting the piles of returned books and carrying them back to the shelves. The stretching motion pulled her blouse taut over her breasts and he yearned to cup their fullness in his hands. His body throbbed with a need so swift and forceful he had to turn away to catch his breath.

"Nick!"

Taken by surprise, her voice was as excited as a child's on Christmas morning, and he turned to see that her brown eyes glowed with unexpected warmth. In an instant, though, she had tempered the display of honest emotion and he almost sighed aloud with disappointment.

"How was your trip?"

Endless, he wanted to say but instead said only, "Fine. Productive."

"Did you get the contract?"

"I won't know for sure until the final papers are in my hand, but it looks that way."

"Congratulations!" She reached out tentatively and touched his arm. "I'm proud of you."

Then, as if the impulsive gesture troubled her, she hurried back toward the desk and began sorting through another stack of books. Nick watched her for several minutes, wondering at the swift return of her nervousness. Finally he followed her and pulled up a chair, turning its back to her and straddling it, his arms propped across the back.

"So, what have you been doing while I've been gone?"

"I've done some more work on the house." Her eyes lit up with enthusiasm. "I found the perfect wallpaper for the bedroom and I'm going to tackle that project next, as soon as I can figure out how to hang the stuff. I'm terrified of getting tangled up in a sheet of paper and winding up glued up like some mummy."

"Want some help?"

Dana promptly looked chagrined. "Nick, I wasn't hinting. You spend all day working on houses. Why should you work on mine in your free time?"

"Because it makes me happy," he said simply. He studied her closely, then promised quietly, "There are no strings attached."

His words, a recognition of what he perceived

as her greatest fear, hung in the silence before she finally said, "I know that. You're not the kind of man who'd attach them."

"I'm glad you're finally able to see that."

Dana hesitated as she seemed to be searching for words. "Nick, my attitude toward you . . . well, it wasn't . . . it isn't personal."

"Meaning?"

"Just that."

"And you don't want to explain?"

She shook her head. "I'm sorry. I really am, but I can't."

He nodded, frustration sweeping through him until he reminded himself that they were making progress. Dana had as much as admitted that trust was growing between them. If he was any judge of her character, he would have to say that the admission had been a giant step for her.

"Shall we talk about your wallpaper instead?" he suggested, adopting a lighter tone. "We could work on it tonight."

She looked tempted but protested anyway. "You're just back from your trip. You must want to get home and see Tony."

"He's not expecting me back until morning and he loves staying with his grandparents. They spoil him, and he'll be furious if I turn up a day early. Now, come on. You can fix me a spectacular dinner while I hang that wallpaper."

Dana still seemed hesitant. Finally, as though

she'd waged a mental battle and was satisfied at the outcome, she smiled. "If you'll settle for something slightly less than spectacular, you've got a deal."

"You've seen my refrigerator. You know I have very low standards. Anything you do would have to be an improvement. Now let's get out of here. I'm starved."

As soon as they arrived at her house, Dana threw potatoes in the oven to bake, tossed a salad and cooked steaks on the grill while Nick measured the wallpaper. He liked listening to the cheerful sounds from the kitchen as he worked. It reminded him of happier times in his past, of coming home to the smell of baking bread and to Ginny, waiting in the kitchen with a smile on her face, anxious to hear about his day. After being without those things for three years, he appreciated all the more Dana's ability to fill a house with welcoming sounds and scents.

He also approved of the simple wallpaper design Dana had chosen. Muted shades of palest mauve and gray intermingled with white in tiny variegated stripes that were both tasteful and easy on the eye. It wasn't frilly and feminine, although that would have suited her, too. It was sophisticated and classy, with just a touch of innocence. As he cut the strips, he chuckled at reading so much into a selection of wallpaper.

Dana already had a bedspread in similar tones

on the brass bed, and matching curtains had billowed in the spring breeze. Nick pulled the furniture away from the walls and had taken down the curtains in readiness for hanging the first strip of paper. As he shifted the bed to the center of the room, he was struck by a powerful sense of intimacy. He felt as close to Dana as if they'd been in that bed together, clinging to each other in the heat of passion.

He could imagine lying there after a night with her in his arms, propped on one elbow, watching as Dana pulled a brush through her long hair. He envisioned all the thousand little things a husband learns about his wife by watching her dress in the morning. His gaze lingered on the pillow as if he could see the indentation from her head, before he finally blinked away the image just in time to hear her call his name from the kitchen.

"Well," she said when they were settled at the table, "are you regretting your impulsive offer?"

"Not a bit. I like to hang wallpaper. When Ginny was alive—" He stopped himself in mid-sentence. "Sorry. I shouldn't do that."

"Do what?" She seemed genuinely mystified.

"I shouldn't keep bringing up my wife."

"Don't be absurd. She was an important part of your life for a very long time. It's natural that you should want to talk about her."

"It doesn't bother you?"

There was a subtle shift in her mood, a hint of

caution in her tone. "No. At least, not the way you mean."

He regarded her curiously, surprised to find her expression almost wistful. "I don't understand."

"I just mean that I wish everyone had a marriage as happy as yours was."

He recalled her comment once before about the social whirl her marriage had entailed and wondered again at the edge in her voice.

"How long were you married, Dana?"

"Five years."

The response was to the point. He sensed she had no desire to elaborate, but he asked anyway, "Do you want to talk about it?"

"No." The response was quick and very firm. "I'd rather leave the past where it belongs."

She retreated again to that place Nick couldn't follow, a place that separated them by both time and distance as effectively as if they still lived in separate worlds. She stared into space and placed her fork back on her plate. Nervously, she drummed her fingers on the table. When he couldn't bear witnessing her unacknowledged pain any longer, Nick put a hand over hers and rubbed his thumb across her knuckles.

"Sometimes that's not possible," he said softly.

Her gaze lifted to meet his, the mournful expression in her eyes painful to see. "It has to be," she said, an unmistakable edge of desperation etched on her face.

Then, as if she'd found some new source of inner strength, she pulled herself together and even managed a faltering smile. "Enough of all that. Surely we can find other things to talk about. Are you finished with your steak?"

"Dana . . ."

"No, Nick. Let it go." The words were part plea, part command. Her demeanor brightened with a determination that awed him a little, even as it worried him.

"I have strawberry shortcake for dessert," she tempted.

He gave in. "When did you have time to fix that?"

"Today. It was no trouble. I had the strawberries and it was easy enough to do the rest. I seemed to remember you like it."

"I love it."

"Would you like to eat on the porch? I think it's warm enough tonight."

"Sounds perfect."

Nick brought out a chair, and Dana settled into her creaking rocking chair. They sat for a long time in companionable silence, letting the night's calm steal over them as they ate.

"Would you like some more?" Dana asked when he'd finished.

"No, please. Another bite and I'll never get off this chair and back to your wallpaper."

"You don't have to do that."

"The matter is settled," he insisted, getting up. "Now come and help me." He held out his hand and pulled her to her feet. She stood gazing up at him, her wide brown eyes searching his face. She tried to withdraw her hand from his, but he held on tightly.

"Dana."

She waited, the only visible sign of her emotions the darkening of her eyes into nearly black pools of pure enchantment. He tried to interpret her expression, but anxiety made him wary of the message he thought he saw. Was it, in fact, a yearning desire or the now familiar trepidation? Never had he felt such uncertainty, such self-doubt. Would the kiss he wanted so badly be welcomed or would it drive her away?

Few things in life came without risks and fewer were more valued than emotional commitment between a man and a woman. True, his feelings for Dana were still too new to be called commitment, yet they tortured him for fulfillment. He stared into her upturned face and slowly, with great care not to frighten her, he lowered his mouth to hers.

It was like touching a match to dry timber. There was an explosion of light and heat. His arms slid around her and this time she accepted the intimacy of the embrace as willingly as she did the kiss. Her hands fluttered hesitantly in the air for no longer than a heartbeat, then settled on his shoulders as a sigh shuddered through her.

The flames burned brighter as memory became reality. His lips caressed her cheeks, sought the strong pulse in her neck and lingered where her perfumed scent rose to greet him. She was soft as silk beneath his plundering mouth, and though she was unresisting he sensed the hesitancy of a new bride. It was the only thing that kept him sane. If he were to let himself go, if he were to give in to the recklessness of his feelings, he knew he might very well lose her forever.

When he released her at last, his breathing was ragged, his pulse racing.

"I think I'd better go, after all. I'll come by the library tomorrow and pick up your keys. I can do the wallpaper while you're at work."

"What about your work?" She was suddenly stiff and distant again. He read regret in her eyes and wondered whether she regretted the kiss or regretted what might have been.

"This should only take a couple of hours and I'm not expected in the office until afternoon."

"Are you sure I'm not imposing?"

He grinned at the worried set to her lips. "You could never impose on me. I want to do this for you."

She nodded then, apparently satisfied, and offered no further protest.

With a second, much quicker kiss on the cheek,

Nick left before he could change his mind, before temptation made him break his unspoken vow to move slowly with Dana, to set a pace that would coax her eventually into his arms.

Dana came home late on Friday, putting off her return to avoid another meeting with Nick in such a private setting. He'd come by the library early, as he'd promised, and even with people around, she'd felt the flaring of impatient desire. It was a sensation she had sworn to resist, but it was getting more and more difficult to do. Her traitorous body craved Nick's touch despite the warnings of her mind.

Now, as she walked through the cottage, it was almost as though she could sense Nick's presence, as though his male scent lingered in the air and his strength surrounded her. In recent days she'd come to trust that strength, rather than fear it, yet old habits were hard to break. Now that she was home, she almost wished that she'd arrived earlier so she could have thanked Nick in person for his efforts.

She found that her room was exactly as she'd envisioned it. The wallpaper was hung, the furniture back in place. Nick had even painted the woodwork. On the nightstand beside the bed, he had left a vase of white and lavender lilacs. The sweet fragrance filled the room. Dana picked them up and buried her face in the fragile blooms, filled with emotions she'd never expected to feel again.

When she put the vase back, she discovered a note.

Dana,
Hope you like the room. Tony and I will be by for you in the morning about eight-thirty. Bring your bathing suit. We're going to the beach.

Until then,
Nick

Her first reaction was annoyance. Once again he was making plans without consulting her, backing her into a corner. Then she reread the note and found that, despite herself, she was smiling, her heart beating a little faster. What woman could stay angry at a man who left flowers in a room he had prepared for her with such care?

That night she slept well for the first time in ages. The next morning she had barely turned over to peer at the clock when the impatient pounding started on the back door.

"Rise and shine, sleepyhead."

"Nick?" Her voice came out in a sleepy croak. She tumbled out of bed and pulled on a robe. She searched for her slippers but finally gave up and walked barefoot to the door.

"You're early," she accused as she opened the

door to a grinning Tony and his very wide-awake father.

"See, Dad, I told you we should've called," Tony said.

From the expression in Nick's eyes, Dana could tell that he wasn't the least bit sorry he'd awakened her. In fact, he looked delighted to see her in her robe, with her hair disheveled and her bare toes curling against the cool floor. She belted the robe a little tighter and stood aside to let them in.

"I thought you said eight-thirty," she said, trying one more time for an explanation for the early arrival.

"I did, but it was such a beautiful day I thought we ought to get an early start." Nick nudged her in the direction of the bedroom. "Go, get dressed. I'll make some coffee. Do you want breakfast?"

"No, but if you want some, help yourselves."

"We've already eaten," Tony chimed in. "Dad fixed waffles. Sort of." He wrinkled his nose in disgust and Dana was immediately intrigued.

"Sort of?"

"Yeah. There's gunk all over the kitchen."

"Quiet," Nick ordered as Dana grinned. "Don't tell her all my bad traits. They tasted okay, didn't they?"

"Heck, yeah. I like charcoal," Tony retorted, ducking as his father took a playful swipe at him.

"Tony, if you want some cereal while you wait,

it's in the cabinet by the stove," Dana offered, laughing.

"The waffles weren't that awful," Nick grumbled.

Impulsively, Dana patted him on the cheek. "I'm sure they weren't, but perhaps you should stick to building houses."

"Somebody in our house has to cook."

"I vote we eat here all the time," Tony said, his voice muffled as he poked his head into the cupboard. "Ms. Brantley's got lots of good stuff."

As Dana's eyes widened, Nick turned and grinned at her. "See, my dear, you have to be very careful what you say around him or he'll be moving in."

Before Dana could come up with a quick retort, Nick added in a seductive purr meant only for her ears, "And where my son goes, I go."

Dana's heart thudded crazily. "I'll keep that in mind," she said, hurrying from the kitchen.

She took her time dressing, trying to regain her composure. Nick always teased her when she least expected it and he had an astonishing ability to unnerve her. She knew he could do that only because she was beginning to lower her defenses. She might as well admit it; Nick was making her feel special. He also made her feel intelligent and desirable again. Their flirting was heady stuff, especially for a woman who'd felt none of those things in a very long time.

"Just don't let him get too close," she murmured as she slipped a pair of jeans on over her bathing suit.

As the day wore on, she found it was a warning that was getting exceptionally difficult to heed.

After riding along a winding road edged by towering pines and oaks they arrived at Westmoreland State Park. They spent the day swimming, walking along the trails, playing volleyball in the water and, finally, cooking hamburgers on a grill.

"Let Ms. Brantley do it, Dad."

"Oh, 'How sharper than a serpent's tooth it is to have a thankless child,' " Nick bemoaned dramatically.

"What?" Tony said.

"That's Shakespeare," Dana told him. "It's a line from *King Lear*."

"What's it mean?"

"It means, my boy," Nick said, "that a kid who is rotten to his old man may not get any birthday presents next week."

"That's a very loose translation," Dana noted dryly.

Tony grinned. "I get it, Dad. You want me to shape up or ship out. How about if I go swimming again?"

"Only if you stay where we can see you. No going out over your head, okay?"

"Promise," he said, taking off across the sand.

When he had gone, Dana and Nick were left alone, sitting side by side on a blanket.

"When is his birthday?" she asked, uncomfortably aware that Nick's bare chest and long, muscular, bare legs were just inches away from her.

"Wednesday."

"Are you doing something special?"

"His grandparents are throwing a party for him." Nick trailed a sandy finger along Dana's bare back, moving back to linger at a tiny ridged scar on her shoulder. She could feel the sensation clear down to her toes. "Want to come with me?"

Dana tried to stay very still so Nick wouldn't see how his touch and his offhand invitation were affecting her. Then she drew her knees protectively up to her chest and folded her arms across them, resting her chin on her hands. She thought about Nick's invitation. It was one more link in the chain to tie her to him.

"I don't think so," she said finally.

"Because you don't want to go?"

She glanced over at him and shook her head. "No, it's not that."

"What, then?"

"I don't think I belong there."

"Why not? The party is for Tony's friends, and as you must know, he thinks you're one of his very best friends." His hand came to rest on her shoulder. "Dana, look at me. Is it because you think Ginny's parents might resent you?"

"That's certainly one reason," she said, struck anew by his perceptiveness and sensitivity.

"They won't. They've been asking for some time when they were going to get to meet you. I thought this might be a good time because there will be a lot of other people there. There won't be so much pressure on you."

"You're sure that's how they feel?"

"Absolutely. But you said that was *one* reason. Are there more?" Before she could reply, he said, "Of course there are, and I'll bet I can guess what they are. You think people will start making assumptions about us if we're seen together on a family occasion."

"That's part of it," she admitted. She hesitated, then took a deep breath. "It's more than that, though. To be honest, I'm also worried about what I'll feel."

"Trapped?"

She met his gaze and saw the guileless expression in his eyes. She nodded.

"You won't be. I'll never try to trap you into more than you're ready for, Dana. Never. This is just a birthday party for Tony."

She thought about what Nick was saying to her and realized that if she was ever to take another chance on letting a man get close to her, Nick was the right choice. She turned and smiled at him. "In that case, I'd love to come."

His gaze met hers and her breath caught in her throat. There was such a look of raw desire, of longing, in his eyes that it made her pulse dance wildly. His hand tangled in her wet hair and he drew her closer. Dana's heart thundered in anticipation, but before the longed-for kiss could happen, Tony's shout drove them apart. He was racing across the sand, tears in his eyes, holding his arm. Nick was on his feet in an instant, tension radiating from him.

"What is it, son?"

Tony looked disgusted. "Just a dumb jellyfish sting," he said, panting from his run across the sand.

"Are you okay?" Dana asked, noting the relief in Nick's eyes.

"Yeah, I'm used to 'em," Tony said bravely, surreptitiously swiping away the tears. "It just hurts a little."

Nick glanced at Dana with regret, then ruffled Tony's hair. "Come on, kiddo. We'd better go see the lifeguard and get something to put on that. Then we'd better think about getting home if you want to go to the early movie with your friends tonight."

When they got back to River Glen, Nick pulled up in front of Dana's house. "How about having dinner with me tonight? We'll go out for crabs."

"I'd like that."

Nick seemed startled by her quick acceptance.

"Terrific. I thought I was going to have to twist your arm."

"Not for crabs. I've discovered an addiction to crabmeat since I moved here."

"Then we'll feed your habit tonight. I'll be by for you about seven."

Dana had butter dribbling down her chin and crab shells in her hair. Nick thought she'd never looked lovelier or more uninhibited. He reached across the table and wiped her chin with an edge of his napkin.

"You're really into this, aren't you?" he said with a grin. "If I'd had any idea cracking crabs was the way to your heart, I'd have brought you here days ago."

Dana didn't even look up. She was concentrating instead on shattering a crab shell so she could get to the sweet meat inside. Newspapers were spread across the table, shells everywhere. Only one of the dozen crabs they'd ordered remained untouched. Nick sipped his beer and watched her pounding away on the next-to-last crab. The shell on the claw finally cracked and she lifted a chunk of tender white crabmeat as triumphantly as if it were a trophy.

"For me?" Nick teased.

She scowled at him. "You get your own. This is hard work."

"And you do it so neatly. If Tony could see this

table now, he'd never again make sarcastic remarks about the messes I leave in the kitchen."

"I suppose you're any better at this."

"As a matter of fact, I am something of an expert," he retorted. "Which you would know if you'd been watching me, instead of smashing your food to bits."

He picked up the last crab and gently tapped it a couple of times. It yielded the crabmeat instantly. He picked up the biggest chunk on his fork, dipped it in butter and held it out for Dana. She hesitated.

"Don't you want it?"

"Oh, I want it. I'm just trying to decide if it's worth the price."

"What price?"

"You'll just sit around looking smug the rest of the night."

"No, I won't," he vowed. "Even though I'm certainly entitled to."

Dana wrapped her hand around his and held it steady while she took the crabmeat off the fork. As she bit down, her eyes clashed with his and held. Nick wondered if she could feel the tension that provocative look aroused. Every muscle in his body tightened.

"Dana," he murmured, his voice thick. She blinked and released his hand. "Dana, I want you."

She met his gaze, then glanced away, her expression revealing the agony of indecision. "I know." She sighed deeply and looked into his eyes again. "Nick, I can't get involved with you. I thought you understood that this afternoon."

"Why do you equate involvement with being trapped?"

"Experience."

"*Past* experience," he reminded her.

"It doesn't matter. I've made decisions about what I want for the rest of my life and involvement isn't included."

"How can you make a decision like that so easily?"

"It's not easy, believe me. Although I thought it would be before I met you."

She hesitated and Nick waited for the rest. "A part of me . . . a part of me wants what you want."

"But?"

"But I can't change the way I am. You have to accept me on my terms."

"Which are?"

"If you care about me, you'll accept that we'll never be any closer than this."

"I'll never accept that!" he exploded, feeling a fury fueled by frustration building inside him. He saw the flicker of fear in her eyes and tried to force himself to remain calm. "I'll give you space, Dana. I'll give you time, but I will never give up hope for us."

"You must." She touched his hand, then jerked away when he would have held hers.

"I can't," he said simply. "That would mean living a lie. I can't do that any more than you can."

"Nick, I don't want to talk about it anymore. My decision is final."

"Sweetheart, nothing in life is ever final," he said softly before calling for the check.

On the way home, Dana sat huddled close to the car door, as if afraid that by sitting any closer to Nick she would be tempting fate. When they got to her house, he walked her to the door, careful not to touch her.

"May I come in?"

She hesitated, then said, "Of course. Would you like some coffee or tea?"

"Tea."

She busied herself at the stove for a few minutes, her back to him. Nick tried to understand the stiff posture, the return of distance when they had seemed so close throughout the day. He knew Dana was afraid, but of what? He was certain it was more than commitment, but nothing he could think of explained her behavior.

"Would you like your tea in here or outside?"

"On the porch," he said, craving the darkness that might lower Dana's resistance, provide a cover for her wariness and make her open up to him.

They talked for hours, mostly about impersonal subjects, until Nick's nerves were stretched to the limit.

"It's getting late, Nick. Shouldn't you be getting home to Tony?"

"Tony's staying at his friend Bobby's tonight and I'm exactly where I want to be." He dared to reach across and clasp her hand. After an instant's hesitation, Dana folded her fingers around his. He heard her tiny sigh in the nighttime silence.

They sat that way until the pink streaks of dawn edged over the horizon, occasionally talking but more often quiet, absorbing the feel of each other. There was comfort just in being together, Nick thought, in seeing in the new day side by side.

And, despite Dana's protests to the contrary, there was hope.

Chapter 6

It was barely ten o'clock in the morning and the temperature in the library had to be over ninety degrees. Dana had clicked on the air-conditioning when she'd arrived at eight. It had promptly given a sickening shudder, huffed and puffed desperately, and died. She'd tried to open the windows, but most of them had long since become permanently stuck. She propped the front door open with a chair, then found an old floor fan in the closet, but it only stirred the humid air. With no cross ventilation, it didn't lower the temperature a single degree.

"Dana, what on earth's wrong in here?" Betsy Markham said, mopping her face with a lace-edged hankie as soon as she crossed the threshold. "It's hot as hades."

"The air conditioner broke this morning. Come on over and sit in front of the fan. It's not great, but it's better than nothing."

Betsy sank down on a chair by Dana's desk and fanned her face with a book. "What did we ever do before the invention of air-conditioning?"

"We sweltered," Dana replied glumly. Then she brightened. "Wait a minute. Betsy, you must know. Do we have a contract for repairs?"

"Never needed one. Nick's always done that sort of thing."

Dana groaned. "I should have known."

"What's that supposed to mean? I thought you two were getting close. Looked that way when I saw you together last week."

"That's the problem. I can't go running to Nick for help again. He's already done way too much for me, especially around the house. I feel like I'm taking advantage of our friendship."

"Land sakes, child, it isn't as if this is some personal favor. This is town property and Nick's always been real obliging about having his crew work on whatever needs fixing. He only charges for parts." Betsy regarded her closely. "You sure

118

that's all it is? You didn't have a fight or some-thing, did you?"

"No. You were right. We've been getting along really well. It scares me sometimes. Nick seems too good to be true."

"He's a fine man."

"I know that's what you think. I think so, too, but can you ever really know a person well enough to be sure of what he's like underneath? What about all those women who wake up one day and discover they're living with a criminal? Or that their husband has three other wives in other cities?"

Betsy looked scandalized. "Goodness gracious, why on earth would you bring up a thing like that? Nick's never broken a law in his life, except maybe the speed limit."

"Do you really know that, though? You're not with him twenty-four hours a day."

Betsy seemed genuinely puzzled by Dana's reservations. "Honey, you're not making a bit of sense. With Nick, well, I've known him since he was just a little tyke. He's always been a little stubborn, maybe a wee bit too self-confident, but you'll never find a more decent, caring man."

The book's pages fluttered slowly, then stopped in midair as Betsy's thoughts wandered back. She shook her head sadly. "Why, the way that man suffered when Ginny was sick, it was pitiful to see. He couldn't do enough for her. Anybody with eyes could tell he was dying inside, but around Ginny he was as strong and brave as could be. He kept that house filled with laughter for her and Tony, and he made sure Ginny's friends felt like they could be there for her. Lots of times when someone's dying, folks don't want to be around 'cause they don't know what to say. Nick put everyone at ease for Ginny's sake. You can tell an awful lot about a man by the way he handles a rough time like that."

Dana felt that wistful, sad feeling steal over her again. "He obviously loved her very much."

Betsy seized on the remark. "Is that what's bothering you? Are you afraid he won't be able to love you as much?"

Dana sighed. "I wish it were that simple, Betsy."

"Then what is it, child? Something's sure worrying at you. Is it Nick who's got you so confused or something else?"

"I can't explain. It's something I have to work out on my own."

"An objective opinion might help."

"Maybe so, but I'm not ready to talk about it."

"Child, sometimes I think you and Nick were meant for each other," Betsy said in exasperation. "You're both just as stubborn as a pair of old mules and twice as independent."

"Betsy." There was a warning note in Dana's voice.

"Okay, I get the message. But if you ever feel

the need to talk, just remember I'm willing to listen and I can keep my mouth shut." Betsy patted her friend's hand. "Now let me call Nick and get somebody over here to work on this air conditioner before you melt right in front of my eyes."

"Thanks, Betsy."

When Betsy had gone, Dana sat staring after her. Their talk had helped her to crystallize some of the uneasiness she'd been feeling lately. She and Nick really had become close. Sometimes it felt as if she'd known him all her life, as if he was a part of her. Occasionally, it seemed he knew what was going on in her mind before she did. That ability to communicate should have reassured her, but it didn't.

When she and Sam had met, they'd shared that same sort of intimacy. A glance was often enough to tell them what they needed to know about the other's thoughts. She had been awed by the closeness back then, but she'd learned from bitter experience not to trust it.

"What you really don't trust is your own judgment," she muttered, disgusted with herself. Nick had done nothing in the weeks she'd known him to betray her trust. People like Betsy, who'd known him since childhood, trusted him implicitly.

But everyone had trusted Sam, too, she reminded herself. He was a well-respected member of a highly prestigious law firm, a devoted son, a supportive brother, a sensitive and generous fiancé. He was all that, but he had been a terrible husband. For reasons she had never understood, he was incapable of dealing with his wife the way he dealt with the others in his life. She had learned that too late. The price for blinding herself to Sam's flaws had been a high one.

"Is the town paying you to sit here gathering wool?" Nick's hands rested on her unsuspecting shoulders. He leaned down to kiss her, but as his lips touched her cheek, Dana trembled.

Nick sat in the chair Betsy had vacated and studied her with troubled eyes. "Hey, I was just teasing. What's wrong?"

"Nothing a little cool air wouldn't cure."

"Coming up," he promised, getting to his feet. He hesitated. Hazel eyes swept over her as if by looking closely he could discover whatever it was she was hiding. "Is that all it is?"

"That's it. Mildew could grow on your brain in this humidity."

"A pleasant thought," he chided lightly as he went to the air-conditioning unit and began dismantling it. "I came over here thinking how lucky I was to get a chance to see my favorite lady in the middle of a workday and you want to discuss mildew."

"I don't want to discuss it. I want the damn air conditioner fixed!"

Nick spun around and stared at her in astonishment. The next minute, tears were streaming down her cheeks and he had her in his arms. "Dana, sweetheart, what is it?"

"I'm sorry," she mumbled against his shoulder.

"Don't be sorry. Just tell me what's wrong."

"Nothing. That's just it. There's nothing wrong."

"You're not making a lot of sense."

"Betsy said the same thing," she said, leaning back in his embrace and looking into his eyes. They were filled with concern and something more, a deeper emotion that she wanted desperately to respond to. She sighed and put her head back against his shoulder. His shirt was damp from her tears and the awful heat, but under-neath his shoulder was solid, as if he could take on the weight of the world.

She wanted so badly to trust what she felt when he held her, but she wasn't sure she dared.

"Dana." He handed her a handkerchief.

"Thanks." She dried her tears and blew her nose. "I don't know what got into me."

"I think you do." Her eyes widened and she started to protest, but he put a finger against her lips. "I'm not going to try to make you tell me today, but someday you must."

She nodded. Maybe someday she would be able to tell him.

By the end of the day she was snapping at her own shadow. She was in no mood to be going to a

123

birthday party at the home of Nick's former in-laws, but she knew a last-minute cancellation would puzzle Nick and hurt Tony.

Fortunately, Tony was so excited he kept up a constant stream of chatter most of the way to his grandparents' home outside of town. Nick kept casting worried looks in Dana's direction, but he maintained an awkward silence, speaking only when Tony asked him a direct question.

Finally, exasperated by the pall that had settled over the car, Tony sank back into his seat and grumbled, "You guys are acting really weird. Did you have a fight or something?"

"Of course not," they both said in a chorus, then looked at each other and grinned.

"Sorry," they said in unison, and chuckled.

Tony gazed from one to the other and shook his head. "Like I said . . . weird. I can hardly wait to get to Grandma's. Maybe there'll be some normal people there. You know, people who'll sing 'Happy Birthday' and stuff."

"You want 'Happy Birthday'?" Nick said, glancing at Dana. "We can give you 'Happy Birthday,' right, Dana?"

"Absolutely."

Nick's deep voice led off and Dana joined in. By the time they pulled into the Leahys' long, curving driveway, there was a crescendo of off-key singing and laughter. Nothing could have lightened Dana's mood more effectively.

Whatever nervousness she'd been feeling about this meeting with Ginny's parents had diminished, if not vanished. Nick squeezed her hand reassuringly as she got out of the car, then draped his arm around her shoulders as they crossed the impeccably manicured lawn to meet the Leahys.

The older couple was waiting on the porch of an old farmhouse. Joshua Leahy's thick white hair framed a weathered face that seemed both wise and friendly. His ready smile deepened wrinkles that had been etched by sun and age. His work-roughened hands clasped Dana's firmly.

On the surface his wife's greeting was just as warm, but Dana sensed an undercurrent of tension.

"We're so glad you could come," Jessica Leahy said, her penetrating brown eyes scrutinizing Dana even as she welcomed her. Dana's own quick assessment told her that Mrs. Leahy had reservations about her but that she was holding them in check for the sake of her son-in-law and grandson.

"I'm glad you're here before the others," she said to Dana. "It'll give us some time to chat before they arrive. Nick, dear, why don't you and Tony help Joshua with the grill? He never can get the charcoal right. Dana, would you mind helping me in the kitchen?"

"Of course not," she said as Nick looked on and gave her a helpless shrug.

In the kitchen, Mrs. Leahy assigned tasks with the brisk efficiency of a drill sergeant. When she was satisfied that Dana was capable of following her directions to finish up the deviled eggs, she picked up a platter of ribs and began brushing them with barbecue sauce.

"So, Dana . . . Do you mind if I call you that?"

"Of course not."

"Well, then, Dana, why don't you tell me about yourself? Nick and Tony think the world of you, but I must admit they don't seem to know too much about your background."

"What exactly would you like to know, Mrs. Leahy?" Dana asked cautiously.

"Oh, where you're from, what your family is like. I find people absolutely fascinating, though sadly we don't get too many strangers settling around these parts."

She tried to make her questions seem innocuous, but Dana had a feeling they were anything but that. Mrs. Leahy had a sharp mind and she had every intention of using her wits to assure herself that her beloved family was not in any danger from the unknown.

"My background's no secret," Dana said as she spooned the egg mixture into the whites and sprinkled them with paprika for extra color. "I'm from New York. My family is still there. My father works for an international bank. My mother raises money for half a dozen charities. I have two sisters, both married and still living in Manhattan."

"You must miss them."

"I do."

"Why did you leave?"

"The pace of the city didn't suit me. I wanted a place to catch my breath, start over."

"Were you running away?"

Dana dropped the spoon with a clatter. "Sorry," she murmured as she bent to pick it up and clean up the egg that had splattered on the gleaming linoleum.

She stood up to find Mrs. Leahy staring at her astutely. "I'm sorry if my question upset you."

"Why should it upset me? I wasn't running away from anything." She met Mrs. Leahy's dubious gaze directly, challenging her. In the end, it was the older woman who backed down and just in time. Nick was opening the screen door and poking his head into the kitchen.

"Mind if I steal the lady for a minute, Jessica? There are some people here I want her to meet."

"Of course, dear. We're almost finished in here anyway." She gave Dana a measured glance. "It was nice talking to you. I'm sure we'll be getting to know each other better."

To Dana's ears, those words had an ominous ring, but then she told herself she was being foolish.

"Sorry about the inquisition," Nick murmured

in her ear as they went into the yard. "Thwarting Jessica's plans is a little like trying to stop an army tank with a BB gun."

"No problem. She's bound to be curious about me."

"Did she unearth any deep, dark secrets I ought to know about?"

Dana frowned. "Why would you ask that?"

"I was only teasing." He studied her closely, an expression of concern in his eyes. "She must have been rough on you."

"Not really," she said, and put her hand on Nick's cheek. Suddenly she needed his strength, needed the reassurance of feeling his warm flesh under her touch. "Don't mind me. I'm just a very private person. It threw me a little to have someone I'd just met asking a lot of questions."

Nick wrapped his arms around her and linked his hands behind her waist. His chin rested on top of her head. Her body was locked against his, and the strength and heat she'd needed were there. Nick embodied vitality and caring, passion and sensitivity, and he was generously offering all of that to her.

With a final reassuring squeeze, Nick released her and took her hand. "Ready to face more people?"

"Do I have a choice?" she muttered. "Let's go."

The rest of the evening passed in a blur of children's laughing faces, introductions and reminiscences, all of which seemed to have Ginny prominently at the center. Dana felt slightly uncomfortable, but Nick appeared downright irritated by what seemed an obvious attempt to keep Dana firmly in place as an outsider.

After he'd dropped an exhausted Tony at home, he drove Dana to her house. "I'm really sorry for the way the evening turned out. I don't understand what got into Jessica tonight. She's not a petty woman."

"She's just trying to protect her family."

"From what?" he exploded. "You? That's absurd. The only thing you've done is bring happiness back into our lives."

"I'm sure that as she sees it, I'm taking her daughter's place."

Nick sighed and bent over the steering wheel, resting his forehead on hands that gripped the wheel so tightly his knuckles turned white. "Ginny is dead."

After a split-second hesitation, Dana reached over and put her hand on Nick's shoulder. "She knows that. That makes it even worse. Why should I be alive when her daughter isn't?"

"You're not to blame, for heaven's sakes."

"She knows that, too. I didn't say her feelings were rational. She may not even be aware of them. It just comes out subconsciously in her actions."

"I'm going to talk to her."

"No, Nick. Let it go. Give her time to adjust.

This must be very hard for her. She doesn't understand that I'm not trying to replace her daughter."

Nick sat back and shook his head. "You're really something, you know that? How can you be so understanding after the rough time you've been through?"

"Don't go nominating me for sainthood," she cautioned with a grin. "There were a couple of times in the kitchen when I came very close to tossing a few deviled eggs at her."

Nick reached across and massaged Dana's neck. "I wish I didn't have to get home right now," he said softly, his eyes blazing with desire.

"But you do," she said, wishing in so many ways it were otherwise, while knowing at the same time that it was for the best. "There will be other nights."

When Dana made that vow, she meant it. She was sure she was prepared to risk taking the next step in her relationship with Nick. Like a wild-flower that beat the odds to survive in a rocky crevice, love had bloomed in her heart. As impossible as it seemed, she was beginning to believe in a future with him.

Then the mail came on Thursday. In it was a letter from Sam's parents. When Dana saw the Omaha postmark and the familiar handwriting, her hands trembled so badly the letter fell to the floor. She stared disbelievingly at the envelope for what seemed an eternity before she dared to pick it up.

How in God's name had they found her? Surely her parents hadn't revealed her whereabouts.

What does it matter now? They know. They know.

It seemed like the beginning of the end of everything she'd worked so hard to achieve. Serenity vanished in the blink of an eye, replaced by pain. Hope for the future was buried under the weight of the past.

Reluctantly, she opened the envelope, daring for just an instant to envision words that would forgive, rather than condemn. Instead, she found the all-too-familiar hatred. The single page was filled with unrelenting bitterness and accusations. All of Sam's parents' pain had been vented in that letter. They promised to see her in hell for what she had done to their son.

What they didn't understand was that she was already there.

Badly shaken, Dana closed the library early and walked home. The arrival of that letter had convinced her that while the Brantleys might not make good on their threats to expose her today or even tomorrow, sooner or later the truth about her past would come out. When it did, it would destroy the fragile relationship she was beginning to build with Nick. She would rather die than see the look of betrayal that was bound to be in his eyes when he learned the truth.

Sitting on her front porch, idly rocking through dusk and on into the night, she decided it would be better to distance herself from Nick. She stayed up all night, and by dawn her eyes were dry and painful from the lack of sleep and the endless tears. She had vowed to end their relationship the next time she saw him. And if Nick wouldn't let her go, she was prepared to leave River Glen.

The next time she saw Nick began with a kiss so sweet and tender it made her heart ache with longing. Nick's lips were hungry and urgent against hers and Dana felt herself responding. Heat spread through her limbs until she was clinging to him. *The last time, the last time,* was like a refrain she couldn't get out of her head, even as her body trembled and begged for more.

At last she pushed him away. Turning her back on him so he wouldn't see the tears welling up in her eyes, she walked into the back room at the library and began unpacking the lunch she'd brought for the two of them.

"We have to talk," she announced.

Clearly puzzled, Nick studied her. "Why so serious?"

Dana took a deep breath and said, "We're spending too much time together."

He stared at her in astonishment. "Where did that come from?"

"It's something I've been thinking about since the other night."

"Since the birthday party."

She nodded.

"I see. Do I have anything to say about the decision or is it unilateral?"

"It's my decision and my mind is made up."

Nick watched her as he peeled a tart Granny Smith apple, then split it and gave her half. "The way I see it," he began slowly, never taking his eyes off her face, "we're not spending nearly enough time together. You and I are going to be together one day. It's as inevitable as the change in seasons. You know it, Dana."

She felt color rise in her cheeks, but she met his gaze straight on and made her tone cool. "I'm not denying the attraction, Nick. I'm just saying that's the end of it. Eventually you're going to want a wife. Tony needs a mother. We've talked about this before. I'm not about to be either of those."

She nearly choked on the words. The ache in her chest was something she would have to live with for the rest of her life.

"Why not?" Nick demanded. "You care for both of us." When she started to protest, he silenced her. "Don't deny it. I know you do and all that nonsense at the Leahys is just that: nonsense."

"That doesn't matter. How many times do we

have to go through this? I've made choices for the rest of my life. You don't fit in. Leave it that way now, before we all get hurt."

"I can't do that, Dana. You're in my heart and there's no way to get you out. I said it the other night and I'll say it again and again until I make you understand: I'll give you time if that's what you need, but I won't leave you alone."

She grasped at straws. "People are already talking about us, Nick."

"Let them."

"That's easy for you. You've lived here your whole life. People respect you. They don't even know me. I don't like being the subject of gossip. It hurts."

"If you're worried about your reputation, there's an easy way to resolve that. Marry me."

Dana's heart pounded and blood roared in her ears, but she forced herself to say, "You're missing the point. Didn't you hear what I said? There will be no marriage, Nicholas. Not for me."

"Was your last marriage such a disaster? Is that it?"

Dana felt something freeze inside her as her thoughts tumbled back in time. Sheer will brought them back to the present.

"I won't discuss my marriage with you," she said, her lips tightly compressed. "Not now. Not ever."

Sound seemed to roar in her head until she

could stand it no more. The hurt look in Nick's eyes was equally impossible to bear.

She clamped her own eyes shut and held her hands over her ears, but she could still see, still hear. "Go, Nick. Please."

"Dana, this doesn't make any sense."

"It does, Nick. It's the only thing that does."

Nick stared at her, his eyes pleading with her to relent, but there was no going back. This was what she had to do. For Nick and Tony. For herself.

But, dear God, how she hated it.

Chapter 7

It was impossible to grow up in a small town without harboring a desire for privacy. The same things that made a community like River Glen so appealing were the very things that could set your teeth on edge. Friendly support could just as easily become outright nosiness. As a result, Nick was a man who understood the need for secrets, and until he had fallen in love with Dana he had been perfectly willing to let each man—or woman—keep his own.

But he sensed there was something different about Dana's secrets, something deeper and more ominous than an understandable need for

135

privacy. Her reluctance to discuss even the most basic things about her marriage, her effort to maintain a distance, the tension-laden silences that fell in the midst of conversation, were all calculated to drive a wedge between them, to prevent him from asking questions about a past she didn't care to reveal.

Though he hated it, for days Nick tried playing by Dana's latest rules. He resumed eating his lunches at Gracie's and spent his evenings at home. He didn't even drive past her house, though there were times when he longed to do just that in the hope of casually bumping into her.

Foolishly, he thought time would make her give in or at the very least make it easier for him. Instead she held firm and it was getting more and more difficult for him to keep his distance. He was lonelier than he'd been since the awful weeks after Ginny's death.

With so many empty hours in which to brood, he even found himself jealous of his own son, who continued to spend his afternoons at the library and came home filled with talk of Dana. Nick listened avidly for some hint that she was as miserable as he was, but Tony's reports were disgustingly superficial and Nick was too proud to probe for more.

It wasn't until the following week when he stopped by town hall that Nick got any real insight into Dana's mood. He walked into Betsy's office and sank down in the chair beside her desk. He removed the hard hat he'd put on at one of his building sites and turned it nervously around and around in his hands.

Betsy glanced up from her typing, her fingers poised over the keys. She frowned at him.

"Nicholas." There was a note of censure just in the way she said his name.

"Morning, Betsy."

She took off her glasses. "You look like a man who could use a cup of coffee," she said more kindly, and went to pour him one. Then she sat back down, folded her hands on her desk and waited.

Nick scowled at her. "You're not going to make this easy for me, are you?"

"Should I?"

"I'm not the one at fault, Betsy, so you can just stop your frowning."

"Is that right?"

He finally swallowed his pride. "Okay, dammit, I'll ask. How is she?" Betsy opened her mouth, but it was Nick who spoke. "And don't you dare ask me who."

She chuckled. "I think I know who you're interested in, Nicholas. I'm not blind."

"Well?"

"Oh, I'd say she looks just about the way you do. Every time I've tried to get her to tell me what happened, she snaps my head off. Maybe you'd like to explain what's going on."

He crossed his legs, propped the hat on one knee and raked his fingers through his hair. "I wish to hell I knew. One minute everything was fine and the next she didn't want to see me anymore. I tried my darnedest to get her to tell me what was wrong, but she kept giving me all this gibberish about needing space."

"Maybe you pushed her back to the wall."

"Is that what she said?"

"She hasn't said a thing. She looked downright peaked when I saw her on Monday, so I went back to the library again yesterday and she was still moping around. I tried to get her to open up, but she just shook her head and said it was something she had to work out on her own. I invited her over to have dinner with Harry and me and she turned me down."

Betsy pursed her lips. "I don't like it, Nick. Dana's hurting about something and it's not good that she's closing out the only folks around here she knows well. She has to talk to someone or she'll explode one of these days. Can't you try to get through to her? Looks to me as though she needs a friend real bad."

"A friend," Nick repeated with a touch of irony.

Betsy reached over and patted his hand. "You always were an impatient man. Being a friend isn't such a bad place to start, Nicholas. Try to remember that."

Nick sipped his coffee to give himself more

time before answering. At last he nodded. "You're right, Betsy. I'll talk to her tonight, if she'll see me."

"Maybe this is one time you shouldn't take no for an answer."

"Maybe so." He bent down and dropped a grateful kiss on her cheek before he left.

All afternoon he tried to plan his strategy. He vowed to unearth the real cause of Dana's sudden retreats, of her obvious fear of commitment. A woman as gentle and generous as Dana would make a wonderful wife and an incredible mother, but each time he stepped over the boundaries she had set—both spoken and unspoken—something seemed to freeze inside her and the chill crept through him, as well.

Nick had the resources to check into Dana's past, but using them offended his innate sense of decency. Confrontation would only send her farther away. The only alternative was to push her gently, to create an atmosphere in which revelations would flow naturally. Nick wondered if he possessed the subtlety necessary for such a tricky task, especially when he felt like cracking bricks in two to vent his frustration.

It was dusk when he walked through town toward the library. As he strolled, he was oblivious to the friendly greetings called out by his neighbors, who stared after him in consternation. All his attention was focused on Dana and the intimidating realization that he was putting his happiness and Tony's at risk by forcing the issue. He tried to remember Betsy's caution that what Dana needed right now was a friend, not an impatient lover.

As he waited for Dana to close the library, he leaned against her car and listened to the calls of bobwhites and whippoorwills as night began to fall. Fireflies flickered and the first bright star appeared in the sky, followed by another and then another, until the blue-black horizon was dusted with them. The air was scented by the sweetness of honeysuckle and the tang of salt spray from the river. It was a perfect night for romance and his body throbbed with awareness.

"Nick!"

Dana's startled voice brought him out of his reverie. He looked up and grinned at her, hoping to get a smile in return. Instead, she wore a frown. She stayed away from him, her arms folded protectively across her chest. Her stance was every bit as defensive as it had been on the day they'd met, and the realization saddened him. How could two people spend so much time together and still be so distant?

"What are you doing here?" she asked warily.

"I thought we should do some more talking."

"Why didn't you come inside, instead of lingering out here in the shadows?"

"I wasn't sure I'd be welcome."

Her shoulders seemed to stiffen at the implied criticism. "The library is public property."

"That's hardly the point," he said gently. "The library is your domain and you made it very clear the other day that my coming there was a problem."

"I'm not sure I'm following your logic. You wouldn't come into the library because it might upset me, but it's okay to lurk around on the street."

"You didn't say anything about the street," he pointed out, hoping to earn even a brief grin from her. She didn't relent.

"It's not just your coming to the library, it's . . . oh, I don't know." She threw up her hands in frustration. "It wouldn't work for us. I was only trying to save both of us from being hurt somewhere down the line. Can't you see that?"

"I don't see how I could hurt much more than I do now. I've missed you."

For an instant he thought a similar cry might cross her trembling lips, but she only said, "Nick, it will pass. You'll meet someone new."

One brow arched skeptically. "In River Glen? I've known everyone here since I was born."

"You could drive to Richmond or Washington if you were all that interested in meeting new people."

He shook his head, dismayed by her cavalier attitude, her willingness to hand him over to some other woman. He felt an explosion building inside, but he fought to remain cool, controlled.

"You just don't get it, do you? You're not some passing infatuation for me. I'm not chasing after you because you're the first attractive woman to move to town in years or the first one to tell me no. I . . ."

He stumbled over saying he loved her, afraid that such a declaration would be too intense for her to handle. Betsy had warned him of just that. "I care about you. You're a very special woman and I don't want to replace you."

"I have to have some space, Nick," she said at last, leaning up against the car beside him and staring into the darkness. "That's what I came here for."

"I've given you space."

Even in the shadows he could see her lips curve in a half smile. "No, you haven't. Until these last two weeks, you've been at the library every day for lunch. You've taken to dropping by my house whenever you like. Do you realize that in the two months I've known you, I haven't finished a single project around either the house or the library on my own?"

"We fixed the roof."

"You fixed the roof."

"What about the bedroom?"

"You did that, too."

"What about the garden? It's flourishing. When I helped you weed it . . ."

"You see? That's just my point. You're taking

over. First the roof, then the bedroom, the garden. There's nothing left that I can point to with pride and say, 'That's mine.' I need that feeling of independence. I need to stand on my own two feet. I can't have you jumping in to do things before I even get a chance to try."

He tried not to show how much the comment hurt. "I thought I was helping."

"I know you did, and you were a help, Nick. There were a lot of things I couldn't possibly have done by myself, even if I'd wanted to, but you didn't even wait for me to ask."

"And that's a problem?"

"It is for me." She swallowed hard, then said quietly, "I don't want to begin to rely on you."

"I don't mind."

"I know you don't. You're a very generous man, but I feel pressured by that generosity."

"I don't mean to pressure you."

Dana sighed. "I know that. It's *me.* It's how I feel. I won't allow myself ever to be trapped by a man again. I won't be dependent on someone else for my happiness."

The revelation took him by surprise, but it made sense. Everything she'd done pointed to a woman crying out for freedom and independence, a woman determined not to repeat some past mistake.

"Tell me about it," he pleaded, desperate for something that would make him understand.

"Why did you feel trapped? Was it because of your marriage?"

"Yes," she admitted with obvious reluctance. "And that's all I'm going to say on the subject."

He reached out to touch her, then withdrew. "It's not enough. I need answers, Dana. More than that, I think you need to give them. You have to deal with whatever it is, then let it go."

"That's what I'm trying to do."

He felt the frustration begin to build again. "By keeping it all inside? You have friends who want to help. Me. Betsy. Let us."

"Can't you just accept the fact that this is the way it has to be and let it go?"

"No." The cornered expression in her eyes had almost made him relent, but he was determined to have this out with her. His vow not to confront her faltered in the face of her resistance. Confrontation now seemed to be the only way to open up a real line of communication. If she still wanted him out of her life, so be it, but he was going to know the reason why. The real reason.

Up to now that reason had been hidden behind her carefully erected facade. All this talk about feeling pressured and needing independence was part of it, but he sensed, as Betsy had, that there was more. Something had triggered those responses in her and apparently it had to do with her marriage.

"Dana, I'm not just being stubborn," he said at last. "Any fool can see that something is eating away at you. Can't you understand how important it is to me to be here for you? I think you and I could have something really special together, but it won't happen if you keep shutting me out. Talk to me. I can be a good friend, Dana, if that's what you need now. I'm on your side."

"This isn't a game where people have to choose sides, Nick." She sighed again. "Oh, what's the use? I knew I couldn't make you understand."

"Say something that makes sense," he retorted. "Then I'll understand."

"Nick, please. I don't want to hurt you. You have been a wonderful friend, but that's all it can be between us."

Dana watched as Nick fought to control his irritation.

"Isn't that what I just said?" he demanded, his voice rising. Dana flinched and felt the muscles in her stomach tense. Then she relaxed as he hesitated, swallowed and said in a more level tone, "Have I ever asked you for anything more?"

"You know you have."

Nick jammed his hands in his pockets in a gesture that had become familiar to her. "If I have, I'm sorry. When we make love, I want it to be what you want, too. I would never knowingly rush you into doing something you weren't ready for. If you want nothing more than friendship now, I'll give you that."

"But you'll go on wanting more. It's there in your eyes every time you look at me."

"It's in your eyes, too, Dana," he said softly.

Only a tiny muscle twitching in her jaw indicated that she'd heard him. She didn't dare linger to examine his meaning too closely. She didn't dare admit that he might be right. She couldn't cope with that explanation for the unending restlessness, for the inability to sleep after an exhausting day.

Ignoring the obvious, she went on determinedly without even taking a breath, "I'm flattered that you feel that way, but it won't work. I can't handle an involvement in my life. Not now. Maybe not ever. You're a virile, exciting man. You deserve more than I can offer."

She reached up, wanting to caress his cheek. Nick's breath caught in his throat, but in the end she drew back. She heard Nick's soft sigh of regret.

"Oh, Nick, please try to understand. You have big plans for the rest of your life," she said. "You can't put those on hold while you wait for me to see if I can deal with a relationship."

"You're at the center of my plans. Do you want to know what I see when I look at the future? I see you and me together forty years from now. We're sitting on the porch of that house of mine, looking at the river, talking, sharing, while a dozen grandchildren play in the yard. I see two people with no regrets, only happy memories."

Tears glistened in her eyes as she listened to his dream, and her heart slammed against her ribs. She wanted that dream as much as he did. It cost her everything to resist the need to walk into his waiting arms, to kiss him until all of her doubts fled.

"It's a beautiful dream, Nick," she said gently. "I wish I could make it come true for you, but it's impossible."

"You keep saying that, but how can I accept it if you won't tell me why?"

"If you care about me as much as you say you do, couldn't you just accept it for my sake?"

Nick searched her eyes and Dana fought the desire to look away, to avoid the pain that shadowed those hazel depths. His shoulders slumped in defeat.

Finally, with obvious reluctance, he asked, "What do you want me to do?"

Hold me, her heart cried. *Fight me on this.*

Aloud all she could say was, "Let me go. Give me some space for now. We can still be friends. Stop by the library if you want, but no more, Nick."

"And Tony? Are you planning to cut him out of your life, too?"

"Of course not. I don't want to hurt him, Nick.

I don't want to hurt anyone. This is the only way to do that. If we keep seeing each other, Tony will want more for the three of us, too."

He gave her a penetrating stare. "What are you afraid of, Dana? Aren't you really scared that you'll begin to feel as much for me as I do for you?"

She met his gaze evenly. "Maybe so," she admitted candidly.

She saw the brightening of his expression and was quick to add, "But that doesn't change anything."

Nick sighed heavily. "Okay, sweetheart, you win." He stood up and dropped a light kiss on her brow. "For now."

When he walked away, he didn't look back.

Dana watched him go, struck anew by his tenderness, by the gentleness that shone through even when he was frustrated and angry. If she'd ever doubted his love before, she did no longer. That love was strong enough to temper fury, resilient enough to withstand pain. It was a love some women never found, deep and true and lasting.

And because a love just as powerful was growing inside her, she had to let him go.

Once again, Nick tried giving Dana the space she claimed to need. In fact, just to prove a point, he gave her even more than she'd bargained for.

It wasn't easy. His body tightened at the memory of her in his arms and he was filled with heated, restless yearnings. If the days were long without the excitement of those midday conversations at the library and the chance meetings around town, the nights were endless.

Irritated all the time, he'd just finished snapping at one of his employees when the private line in his office rang.

"Yes, hello," he barked.

"Nicholas, dear, I hate to bother you at work, but I need to see you," Jessica Leahy said, her voice taut. The tension in her greeting was enough to worry him and to temper his tone.

"Is there some problem, Jess? Is Joshua okay?"

"Joshua's fine, but we need to talk."

"It sounds urgent."

"I think it may be. Could you come by this afternoon?"

He didn't hesitate for an instant, despite his recent irritation with Jessica. He'd always loved his wife's family. They'd begun treating him like the son they'd never had long before he and Ginny had married. Since her death, they had remained close, growing even more so because of Tony. The only time he could ever remember growing impatient with Jessica was on the night of Tony's birthday party. Thanks to Dana's insights, he'd even come to understand her uncharacteristic behavior that night.

"I'll be there in a half hour."

When he arrived, his mother-in-law was sitting on the porch in her favorite rocker staring off into space, the rocker idle. Her figure as trim as a girl's, she was wearing jeans and a Western-style plaid cotton shirt. But despite the casual attire, every white hair was in place, her makeup flawless. There was a silver tray with a pitcher of iced tea with lemon and mint beside her. She was the picture of serenity, except for one jarring note —she was absentmindedly twisting a handkerchief into knots.

She watched him come up the walk with troubled eyes. When he'd perched on the porch railing beside her, she poured him a glass of tea and took her time adding the lemon and mint as if she wanted to postpone their talk as long as possible.

"I know how busy you are, Nicholas, so I'll get right to the point," she said finally. "How much do you know about this Brantley woman?"

Nick flinched at her phrasing. It implied that a judgment had been made, that Dana had been found wanting in some way. He took a slow, deliberate sip of the tea before he spoke. "All I need to know."

"I don't think so," she said, her tone curt to the point of rudeness. Her shrewd eyes assessed him. "Are you in love with her?"

"Yes."

As if his quick response pained her, she closed her eyes for an instant, then said softly, "I was afraid of that."

Nick exhaled sharply. So that was it. She was going to pursue this illogical campaign to discredit Dana in his eyes.

"She's a lovely young woman," he said gently. "I think if you gave her half a chance, you'd like her."

"I thought perhaps I could, too, but now I'm not so sure. There are some rumors going around." At his indignant expression, she held up her hand. "I know, Nicholas. I'm not one for gossip, either, but I think you'd better look into this. If it's true, then I think you should keep Tony away from her."

"What the devil are you talking about?" Nick said, getting to his feet and beginning to pace. The creaking boards under his feet only increased his agitation. He stared at Jessica incredulously. "There couldn't possibly be anything about Dana that would make me want to keep Tony away from her. She's absolutely wonderful with him. And he adores her."

"I'm very much aware of that. He talks about her all the time. That's why I'm so concerned. If she's to be a big influence on his life, I want to be sure she's a fit person. He's my only grandson, Nick. I want what's best for him."

"This is ridiculous. Of course she's fit. How

can you even suggest something like that? Is it Ginny? Would you feel the same way about any woman?"

"Perhaps so, but I like to think not." Her expression softened and she caught his hand as he stood beside her. "Darling, I'm not just being jealous on my daughter's behalf. Honestly I'm not."

She waved aside his attempt to interrupt. "Wait a minute, please. I know that's the way it must have seemed the other night. Joshua read me the riot act over my behavior. I don't need you to do it, too. Ginny would be the first one to want you to be happy again. But if these things I've heard about Dana Brantley are true, I don't think this woman's the right one for you. If it were just you, perhaps I wouldn't be so concerned. You're a grown man. You can make your own choices, your own mistakes. But there's Tony to consider, too. He's just an impressionable boy. I should think that would be important to you, as well."

"Dammit, you're being cryptic, and it's not at all like you to make judgments about people without giving them a chance. If you think you know something about Dana, tell me."

"I don't *know* anything. All I've heard is the gossip."

"Gossip that's usually nothing but half truths."

"An interesting choice of words, Nicholas.

Half truths. Don't you deserve to know if there's any truth at all to the rumors? Find out about Dana Brantley's past. That's all I'm asking you to do. If she has nothing to hide, she'll tell you and that will be the end of it."

Suddenly the secrets and silences came back to haunt Nick. For the first time, he was genuinely afraid. If he probed too deeply, what would he find? Would it be the end for him and Dana?

Chapter 8

Thunder rumbled ominously as Nick drove away from his mother-in-law's house. Dark clouds rolled in, dumping a torrential rain in their wake. Troubled by his meeting with Jessica, Nick went to his favorite spot overlooking the river, parked under a giant weeping willow and sat staring at the water through the rain that lashed at the windshield. Usually the serenity of the Potomac soothed him, but today the storm-tossed water churned in a way that mirrored his emotions.

Why hadn't Jessica told him about the rumors and been done with it? But even as he asked himself the question, he knew the answer. She was not the type of woman to spread hurtful gossip. Whatever she'd heard about Dana must have been terribly convincing, and very damning, for her even to mention it. But for the life of him, he couldn't imagine Dana ever having done something for which she might be ashamed.

"We all make mistakes," he muttered aloud, thinking of Dana's silences. "We all do things we regret." As wonderful as he thought Dana was, she wouldn't be human if she hadn't made some mistakes in her life. Whatever hers might have been, he believed they could deal with them if they could only get them out in the open.

Dreading the task before him, Nick drove back to his office and called the library. It had been days since he and Dana had talked, and he had no idea what sort of reception she would give him. Dana answered on the fifth ring, her voice breathless and edgy.

Nick was immediately alert. "Hey, are you okay?" he asked. "Is something wrong?"

There was a long silence.

"Dana, what's going on over there?"

He heard her take a deep breath, as if she were drawing in the strength to speak.

"Nothing, Nick," she said finally. "I'm fine. I was up on a ladder in the back when the phone rang. It took me a minute to get here. That's all."

"I see."

This time he was the one who hesitated for so long that Dana eventually asked, "Did you want something, Nick?"

"Yes. Dana, could I see you tonight? There's something I think we should talk about."

More guarded silence greeted the suggestion. At last, she said wearily, "Nick, we've been through everything."

"Not this."

"No. It's not a good idea."

"Dana, please. It's important. We could go to a movie."

"I thought you wanted to talk."

"I do. We can stop for coffee afterward." What he didn't say was that he wanted to prolong their time together, that sitting beside her in a movie would at least give him the temporary illusion of the togetherness he'd missed so much. It would also put off a conversation that was likely to have a profound impact on their future.

"How bad could it be spending a few hours together?" he coaxed. "It's even that George Clooney movie you've been wanting to see. Remember we talked about going?"

There was a heavy sigh of resignation. "Is this going to be like bingo? Are you just going to badger me until I give in?"

"Probably."

He thought he'd detected a glimmer of amusement in her voice, but it was gone when she answered. "Okay," she agreed with such obvious reluctance that it hurt as much as an outright rejection.

"I'll pick you up at six-thirty," he said. "We'll go to the early movie."

"Couldn't I just meet you there?"

Nick closed his eyes. "Why, Dana? Are you that afraid to be alone with me?"

There was a sharp intake of breath and this time there was real emotion in her voice. "Oh, Nick, I'm sorry if that's what it sounded like. Of course I'm not afraid to be with you."

"Fine. I'll pick you up at six-thirty, then."

Nick held the receiver for a long time after Dana had hung up, irrationally unwilling to break the connection. From that moment until six-fifteen, when he left his house after showering and shaving and sending Tony off with grand-parents, he tortured himself over the questions he'd have to ask. He felt like a traitor for wanting to know about a past Dana clearly wanted to forget. He'd been expecting trust from her. Didn't he owe her as much?

When he arrived at her house, he was dismayed to see that the circles under her eyes were darker than ever. Her complexion had a gray cast to it despite the attempt to heighten her color with a touch of blusher. Her slacks hung loose, as if she'd lost weight just since he'd seen her last. Despite his worry, Nick's pulse raced with abandon. His body tightened and he had to resist the urge to draw her into a protective embrace.

As they drove through town, she said, "We

could skip the movie and just get this over with."

He glanced at her, saw again the obvious signs of tension and exhaustion, then shook his head. "No. I think we both can use the relaxation."

She shrugged indifferently and settled back in the bucket seat. It took only a few minutes to reach the town's single theater, but the thick silence between them made it seem like hours. Tension seemed to have wrapped itself around Nick's neck, cutting off his voice. He was grateful they were a few minutes late and had no time to talk as they found seats in the already darkened theater.

The movie passed in a blur as his own reel played in his mind. He recalled Jessica's behavior on the night of Tony's party and again this afternoon. He had no doubt that her concern was genuine, but he was equally convinced it was unwarranted. Still, with Tony's welfare at stake, he had no choice but to explore her veiled charges about Dana.

He gazed at Dana, who sat stiffly next to him, and wondered how things had gone so terribly awry between them. Faced with the uncertainty of their situation, the tension inside him built. He felt as though he were out with a distant stranger, instead of the warm, giving woman with whom he'd fallen slowly but inevitably in love.

When the lights came up, Dana blinked and Nick realized she, too, had been lost in thought.

"Maybe we should stay for the next show," he suggested wryly. "I don't think either of us saw this one."

"I doubt it would help. I think we both have too much our minds."

"Shall we go, then? Maybe we can unburden ourselves."

"Talking doesn't work miracles," she said with a note of regret.

"Maybe not, but it's a start."

He got to his feet and Dana followed. As they walked out into the deepening twilight, Nick saw two old friends. He'd known Ron Barlow and Hank Taylor since childhood, and though he had no desire to stop and chat with them now, he felt he couldn't ignore them.

"Do you mind, Dana?" he said, gesturing in their direction. "We should go over and say hello. Hank does a lot of subcontracting work for me. Ron is a vice president at the bank. The three of us used to bowl together with our wives when Ginny was alive."

"Maybe you should speak to them alone. I might make them uncomfortable."

"Don't be silly. Come on." He slid an arm around Dana's waist and steered her in their direction.

"Hey, Ron. Hank." He patted Ron on the back and shook hands with Hank. "Did you enjoy the show?"

"It wasn't bad," Ron mumbled awkwardly just as his wife, Lettie, came up and linked an arm through his. She didn't look at Nick at all, just whispered to Ron and hurried him away before Nick could even introduce Dana. Hank and his wife followed, though Hank shot a look of regret over his shoulder as they left.

"I don't understand," Nick apologized, staring after them in confusion. He gazed into Dana's eyes and saw the hurt she was trying so hard to cover. He searched for an explanation that made sense. "Maybe they're like Jessica. Maybe they're thinking about Ginny."

"Maybe so," Dana said tiredly.

The whole thing was a thoroughly disconcerting experience for a man who'd always made friends easily and usually commanded fierce loyalty from all who knew him. But tonight it was as though he and Dana were being intentionally shunned without knowing what they had done to deserve it.

No, he reminded himself. Dana might very well know why attitudes had changed so abruptly. Jessica certainly thought she did. That was what this evening was all about: putting an end to the secrets and evasions.

Even though she might know the cause, Dana seemed every bit as disturbed as he was by the whispers and covert examinations.

"Shall we stop by Gracie's for coffee and pie?" he suggested.

"No. We can talk just as well at my place," she said, staring after a woman who'd just ignored her greeting. It was evident to Nick that she didn't want to deal with another such rejection. By the time they got back to her house, she was badly shaken. He would have felt better if she'd simply been angry. Instead, she acted as though there was no fight left in her.

She poured them both a glass of iced tea, but her hand was trembling when she handed Nick his. Then she took up pacing around the kitchen. At last she asked, "Am I crazy or were people avoiding us tonight? Not just those two couples but everyone?"

"I'm sure it was just your imagination," he said, but his voice lacked conviction.

"What about your imagination? Was it getting the same impression?"

"There's probably some perfectly logical explanation. Maybe I just split the seat out of my pants and no one dared to tell me."

Dana glowered at him. "Don't try to make a joke out of this, Nick. Something's very wrong. Everyone's been very friendly to me since I arrived in town—until tonight. Have you heard any rumors going around?"

"What sort of rumors?" he hedged.

"I don't know. It seems around here buying a new dress is cause enough for gossip."

Nick's eyebrows arched at the sarcasm. "I've

never heard you sound bitter before. Is it what happened tonight or is it something more? Have there been other incidents you haven't mentioned to me?"

Dana stopped her pacing to declare, "I'm just fed up with people digging around in my life. I came here to escape that. I should have known it would be worse than ever in a place like this." Angrily, she clenched her hands into tight fists. Nick reached out and caught one hand in his and rubbed his thumb across the knuckles until her grip relaxed.

"Come on," he urged. "Sit down. Let's talk this out. There has to be some reasonable explanation."

She yanked her hand away and began pacing again. "I can't sit down. Do you have any idea what it's like to feel people staring at you, making judgments about you, especially people you thought were your friends? It's awful," she said, her voice rising at first in outrage, then catching on a sob.

She stared at Nick and her mournful expression almost broke his heart. She sat down and put her head in her hands.

"I thought it was over," she said, her voice muffled. "I thought it couldn't follow me here, but it has."

Nick seized on the remark. "What has followed you? Dana, what are you talking about? What rumors could there be?"

She looked up and stared at him blankly, as if she'd been unaware of the full implications of what she'd said, then she shook her head. "Never mind."

"Dana, stop hiding things from me. I care about you. Please, can't you talk to me about what's worrying you? There's nothing you can't tell me. I promise you I won't make judgments."

Her lips quivered, but her voice held firm. "I can't, Nick."

"Why? Why can't you tell me, dammit? You know I'm not just being nosy."

Tears trickled down her cheeks and she bit her lips.

"Dana?"

When she still didn't respond, he slammed his fist down on the table and Dana's eyes widened in fear. "For God's sakes, Dana, talk to me. Fight back."

She shuddered, then squared her shoulders determinedly. "You can't help, Nick. I can't even help myself." Her eyes were empty, her voice expressionless. "Go on home. I just want to go to bed."

"Dammit, I am not leaving you alone when you're this upset. You're shaking, for heaven's sakes." All thoughts of his planned confrontation vanished now as he responded to her pain. "Dana, please, let me help you."

"I'll be fine," she insisted. "Go home to Tony."

"Tony's with his grandparents tonight. You're the one who needs me. I'm staying right here."

Dana apparently saw the implacable look in his eyes, because she finally shrugged and gave in. "Okay, fine. Stay if you like. You can sleep in the guest room."

With that she whirled around and left him alone at the kitchen table wishing he had some idea how to comfort her. But how could you offer comfort to a woman who refused to admit she needed it? Dana was all stiff-necked pride and angry determination. By hinting that he sensed a weakness, a vulnerability, he had forced a denial. She had virtually rejected him, as well.

He listened to the simple, routine sounds of Dana getting ready for bed: the water running, drawers opening and closing, then finally the rustle of sheets. Vivid images played across his mind, taunting him. When he could no longer see a light under the bedroom door, he tiptoed down the hall and stood outside her room, certain he could hear the choked sound of her muffled sobs.

"Dana."

Only silence answered him.

Dana bit her lip to keep from responding to Nick's call. Hot, salty tears slid down her cheeks and dampened the pillow. They were tears for a past she couldn't forget and a present she couldn't prevent from whirling out of control. Her arms ached from the effort it had cost her to keep from throwing them around Nick's waist and holding on for dear life. His strength could get her through this, but she didn't dare begin to count on it. Far more than pride had held her back. She loved him. No matter how she had angered him, how deeply she had hurt him, he had given her gentleness and understanding. She couldn't give him more heartache in return.

A fresh batch of tears spilled down her cheeks. Dear God, how she needed him, but she had to be strong enough to let him go. Tonight after the movies, feeling the stares burning into her, she had seen more clearly than ever that it was the only way. She couldn't embroil Nick in her problems, not when those problems seemed to be mounting every minute. She'd only be an albatross to a man who might one day want to run for office. She and Nick had never discussed his political aspirations, but she'd heard about them. He deserved the chance to make a fine legislator.

She swallowed another sob and clung to her pillow, pretending it was Nick she held. She tried to imagine his strength seeping into her. With him by her side, she could face almost anything. Without him, it was going to be hell all over again.

She heard the creak of the ancient bedsprings in the guest room and it sent a shiver down her spine. *You could be with him,* she told herself. *All you have to do is walk down the hall, go to him. He won't turn you away.*

But it wasn't nearly that simple and she knew it. In the morning she would find the strength to say goodbye again and convince Nick that this time she really meant it.

Nick woke before dawn, and after hesitating indecisively in the hallway, he opened the bedroom door and crept in to check on Dana. The dim light from the hall cast the room into patches of golden brightness and dim shadows.

Dana was in the middle of the bed in a tangle of sheets, her nightgown of silk and lace twisted midway up her thighs. She was sleeping soundly now, though he had heard her restless tossing for most of the night. He tiptoed closer and sat down carefully on the edge of the bed.

She looked so peaceful and vulnerable lying there, her hair flowing over her shoulders in rich brown waves, her skin slightly damp and flushed from the summer night's heat. He brushed the hair back from her face, then lingered to caress her cheek. Even in sleep, a responsive smile tilted the corners of her mouth. Unable to resist, he leaned down to press a kiss on her lips. They were like cool satin beneath his touch, smooth and resilient.

Dana sighed at the touch of his mouth on hers and Nick deepened the kiss, lingering to savor the sensations it aroused, to delight in her sleepy responsiveness. His hand drifted down to skim over her bare shoulder, then slid the thin strap on her gown aside. His thumb followed the curve of her jaw and his tongue tasted the soft hollow of her throat. She stirred restlessly and he tried to soothe her by gently stroking her arm.

Suddenly, as if trapped in the midst of a waking nightmare, she sat straight up in bed. Her eyes snapped open and stared around in unseeing terror. Her hands were thrown protectively up in front of her. Her whole body shook violently.

"No, please. No."

The words were a desperate whimper that stunned Nick into silence as she frantically drew the sheet up like a protective shield, clutching it around her and huddling in a corner of the bed.

Finally, his thoughts whirling, he forced himself to speak. He had to break through this blind panic.

"Dana, love, it's me. Nick. It's okay. I'm not going to hurt you." His voice was low and soothing. He spoke steadily, despite the pounding of his heart and the fear unleashed inside him. "Shh, sweetheart, it's okay. Nobody's going to hurt you."

She blinked as his words began to register. "Nick." Her eyes seemed to focus. The fear seemed to slowly dissipate, but not the trembling.

"Darling, I didn't mean to frighten you. Can I hold you?" he asked softly, reluctant to make another move without her approval.

She sat rocking, wrapped in the sheet, her arms around her stomach, her gaze locked on some awful, distant memory.

"Dana?"

At last she nodded. "Please."

As Nick's arms went around her, one last shudder swept through her and she curved herself into his comforting warmth. Then her tears began. They flowed endlessly. She wept until he thought both their hearts would break.

Chapter 9

Dana clung to Nick, her whole body shuddering with deep, wrenching sobs brought on by the unexpected reawakening of old wounds. Nick's gentle kiss had plucked her from a lovely dream and cast her into a nightmare he couldn't possibly have anticipated. Yet despite the seemingly irrational violence of her reaction, he continued to soothe her, his hands gently massaging her back, brushing the hair from her face.

"It's okay, love. It's going to be okay," he promised, and because she needed to, she believed him.

His words soothed her like a balm until at last she was still, totally drained by the experience. She drew in a deep breath and tried to pull free, but Nick held her still. For once, she hadn't the strength to resist. She burrowed her face in the male-scented warmth of his shoulder, while his arms circled her, lending strength and comfort. His steady breathing and slow, constant heartbeat were like the rhythmic sounds of a train, lulling her.

For this brief moment in time Dana felt safe, as if no harm could ever come to her again. She knew all too well, though, how fragile and fleeting that feeling could be.

"Feel better?" he asked.

She nodded, unable to trust her voice. Deep inside lurked the fear that if she opened her mouth at all, it would be to scream with such agony that Nick would flee just when she was discovering she needed his steadiness and quiet calm the most. Already she'd shown him a side of her she'd hoped he would never encounter. She could only begin to imagine what he must think of her after her unintentional display of histrionics, yet he hadn't run.

"I'm sorry," she said finally.

"There's nothing to be sorry about," he said, giving her a reassuring squeeze. "I'm the one who should be apologizing. I obviously frightened you. I guess I wasn't thinking. You looked so peaceful while you slept, so beautiful, that I couldn't resist kissing you. When you kissed me back, I wanted more. I shouldn't have given in to the feeling. I should have realized you'd be startled."

Surprisingly, she felt her lips curve into a half smile. "I think that's a slight understatement. You must have thought I was demented."

"Hardly."

She felt his fingers thread through her hair. When he reached her nape he massaged her neck until the knots of tension there began to unwind, replaced by a slow-spreading warmth that settled finally in her abdomen. Desire, dormant for so long, flared at his touch. She felt alive again and, despite everything, hopeful. She relaxed into the sensations, allowing her enjoyment of Nick's seductive caresses to last far longer than was wise.

Just a few minutes, she said to herself. *Just let me have a few minutes of solace in the arms of a man I love. Let me feel again, just for a little while. Surely that's not asking too much.*

"Dana, talk to me about your marriage. What went wrong?"

The seemingly innocent request snapped her out of her quiet, drifting state. Her muscles tensed immediately and her heart thumped so loudly and so hard she was sure the sound must echo through the bedroom.

She shook her head. "I can't talk about it."

"You must. I finally realize that must be what has been standing between us from the beginning. It's the only thing it could be."

"Nick, please. Let the past stay buried."

"I wish that were possible, but it's obviously not. Just look at your reaction this morning."

She stiffened and her tone became defensive. "That's a pretty big leap in logic. What makes you think that has anything to do with my past? Any woman who normally lives alone would be startled to find herself being attacked while she's still half-asleep."

His brow lifted at her choice of words. "Is that what it was?" She heard the doubt in his tone, saw it in his eyes, and suddenly she couldn't bear to go on with the facade a minute longer. Nick truly cared about her, perhaps even loved her, though he'd never said the words aloud. She'd seen the emotion, coupled with desire, time and again in his eyes. At the very least he deserved the truth, no matter how difficult the telling of it might be for her.

Sighing in resignation, she met his gaze. "What do you want to know?"

"How did you meet your husband?"

"We were in college together. He was a few years older. He was already finishing law school just as I started undergraduate school. We met at a fraternity party."

"Did you marry right away?"

"No. We waited until he'd finished school and gone to work."

"Were you happy?"

"In the beginning, yes. We were very happy."

"But not always?"

"No."

"What happened? Did he start running around with other women? Spend too much time at work?"

"Why are you so sure that I'm not the one at fault?"

"Because it's very clear that commitment is not something you take lightly. You'd fight for your marriage."

"Yes," she said very softly. "I suppose, in a way, I did."

A thousand images from those five long years flashed through her mind. The mental album began with Sam as he'd looked on their wedding day, his gray eyes watching her with pride, shining with love. She recalled vividly the nights of glorious passion, when his slightest touch fired her blood. Then there were the pictures of Sam at an endless series of parties, her arm tucked possessively through his, or Sam staring hard at her every second they were separated in a room as if in search of the slightest hint of betrayal. And then . . . She shut her eyes against the images of what happened next, but the visions stayed with her, burned indelibly in her memory.

Nick's arms tightened around her. "Tell me, love. Maybe talking it out will help." His breath whispered across her bare shoulder.

Dana had also once thought that talking was an

answer. She had tried to talk to her family, but they'd turned a deaf ear. They'd been so impressed with her perfect marriage to a man they admired that they hadn't wanted to listen to the flaws. Her sisters had their own problems just trying to make ends meet. They couldn't understand how anyone with Sam's and Dana's financial resources could possibly be troubled.

The next time she'd dared to talk it had been to a psychiatrist, and by then it had been too late for anything to help. There was no reason to believe that opening up to Nick would bring her anything but more pain. She was so afraid of the expression she would see in his eyes when she'd finished. Pity, doubt or condemnation would be equally difficult to bear.

"Oh, Nick," she murmured in a tone that decried his innocence. Would he ever fully understand how truly fortunate he had been in his own marriage? How rare the unselfish joy he had found with Ginny was?

"You want to know what went wrong in my marriage, as if it were possible to pick out a single moment and say, 'Ah, yes, that's when it began falling apart. That's what all the arguments were about.' It doesn't work that way. The disintegra-tion takes place in stages, so slowly that you don't always recognize it when it begins to happen and the cause may have very little to do with the symptoms."

Nick shook his head in denial. "I can't accept that. Maybe you can't see it at the time, but now, in retrospect, surely you can."

"Not really, and believe me, I've tried and tried. I kept hoping I could pinpoint the start of it so I could understand it myself. We had arguments at first, like any newly married couple trying to adjust. They were always over little things. I squeezed the toothpaste from the bottom, Sam squeezed it from the top. I left my pantyhose hanging in the shower. He dropped his socks on the bedroom floor. Was that when it began? Did it fall apart over toothpaste, pantyhose and socks?"

She looked to Nick for a comment, but he simply waited. "Okay, maybe it was the first time he dumped an entire meal on the dining room floor because I'd fixed something for dinner he didn't like. Or maybe it was the first time he accused me of paying too much attention to one of his coworkers at an office party. Maybe, though, it wasn't until the night he slapped me for challenging his opinion in public."

Her tone took on an edge of belligerence. "Which time do I pick, Nick? Which time was just your normal, everyday marital squabble and which was the first sign that my husband was sick, that he was unable to cope with pressure and that I was likely to become the target for his anger?"

Nick swallowed hard as the implication of that

sank in, but his gaze was unblinking, compassionate and unrelenting. "Go on."

Dana shivered in his arms and closed her eyes against the memories again, but as before, that only seemed to focus them more sharply.

She spoke in a voice barely above a whisper, fighting against the sickening tide of nausea that always accompanied her recollections.

"I remember the first time Sam hit me. I was so stunned." Even now her voice was laced with surprise. "I had known he was upset. His anger had been building for weeks. The pressures at work were getting worse and he was tense all the time. One night he just snapped. It was over what I'd considered a minor disagreement in public. When we got home, he started yelling at me about it. All of a sudden he was practically blind with rage. After he hit me, he cried. I sat on the bed with this red mark on my face and Sam kneeling on the floor beside me, crying, apologizing, promising it would never happen again, begging me to forgive him."

She looked up and saw tears shimmering in Nick's eyes. She had to turn away. His pity was unbearable.

"But it did happen again, didn't it?" he said softly.

She shrugged, trying to appear nonchalant. "That's the pattern, isn't it? The first time, the husband apologizes and the wife believes him and things do get better . . . for a while. Then it happens again." She pressed her hands to her face. "God, I was so ashamed. I kept thinking it must be my fault, that if only I were a better wife he wouldn't be doing this. I tried so hard not to do anything that might set him off, but it seemed as though the quieter and more amenable I became, the more outraged he was."

"Did he drink?"

"Sometimes. He knew he couldn't handle it, so usually he stayed away from liquor. It was always much worse when he'd been drinking. I used to turn down drinks, hoping that he wouldn't take one, either, but it didn't work. It just meant I was sober enough to watch while he got drunk, knowing that sooner or later he was going to take it out on me. Sometimes he would come home very late, after I had gone to bed, and he would wake me up. . . ."

She choked back a sob and put her hands in front of her face. "He . . . he would wake me up and . . . Oh, God, Nick, I felt so violated. It was like being raped by some horrible stranger."

Nick's breath caught in his throat. "Oh, my God." The words seemed to be wrenched from somewhere deep in his soul. "It was like that this morning for you, wasn't it? No wonder . . ."

"No, Nick. It wasn't like this morning," she said, reaching up to tentatively caress his cheek. She couldn't let him equate his tenderness with

175

Sam's ugly violence. "You were gentle, not like Sam. It's just that when I first woke up I was disoriented. For a minute . . ."

"For a minute you thought it was happening all over again."

Dana nodded. She felt Nick's hand on her shoulder, warm and comforting as it tried to counter the chill that swept through her.

"I am so sorry, Dana. So very sorry."

"So am I," she said, her voice laced with bitterness. "But do you realize how many women go through exactly what I did? Some sources say around thirty percent. One out of every three women will be abused at some time by a man in her life, a husband, a boyfriend. Not just me. I couldn't believe it when the psychiatrist told me. I had been so sure I was all alone."

Nick drew her more snugly into his arms and held her. She felt his tears run down his cheek and mingle with hers. He rocked her back and forth, murmuring softly. She was hardly aware of what he was saying, just the soothing sound of his voice washing over her, trying to ease the pain.

Finally he loosened his embrace and brushed away her tears. She remembered being frightened of those hands, terrified of their strength, but now she felt only their gentleness.

"I want you to listen to me for a minute," he said. "I know that what you experienced was awful. I can't even begin to imagine how horrible it must have been for you, but that was Sam. Not me. It's over now. I can understand how you would be wary of men. In fact, a lot of things make sense to me now: your fear of getting close to me, your defensiveness, your need for independence. But, Dana, you can't build a wall around yourself and live the rest of your life in isolation."

"You're wrong," she replied wearily. "It's the only way I can live."

"Dana, I'm not like Sam Brantley. Don't you know I would die rather than harm you? What we have is special and good. We owe it to ourselves to give it a chance."

"I know that's what you want and on one level it's what I want. Intellectually I can tell myself that you and Sam are very different men, but emotionally I can't convince myself of that. There are too many scars." Nick flinched and she reassured him. "Not physical scars, psychological ones. They're just as long-lasting. I don't know if I'll ever feel totally comfortable around men again."

"Even after all these weeks, can't you see you can trust me?"

Dana heard the hurt in Nick's voice, but once started, she had to tell him the truth. She touched his cheek with regret as she said, "No, I can't."

"But—"

"No, wait. This isn't something that's your

fault, Nick. Without living through it, you can't possibly understand what abuse like that does to your ability to trust your own judgment," she countered.

She searched for words to make Nick understand the inexplicable. "My husband was attentive, kind and loving all during our courtship. He was an educated man with an excellent career. That's the man I fell in love with, but there was a dark side to him, a side I never saw before we were married. Maybe he hid it. Maybe I blinded myself to it. I'll never really know.

"You talk about the weeks we've shared. Remember, Sam and I had known each other for three years in college, and I still hadn't guessed that he was capable of violence. Sam would pick up an injured animal from the side of the road and take it to a vet. He was a soft touch for any sob story. How could a man like that possibly be abusive to another human being, especially his own wife?"

"I still don't understand why you didn't leave him once you did know, why you subjected yourself to more suffering."

"There are so many reasons a woman doesn't leave. For some it's the children."

"But you didn't have that problem."

"No, because I refused to get pregnant by a man with no control over his anger. We had some horrible fights over that. Sam wanted kids.

We'd planned for them, but when the time came for me to stop using birth control, I couldn't go through with it. I even tried to use that as leverage to make him get help, but it was as if he had no idea why I thought he needed it."

"Then I'll ask you again. Why did you stay?"

Dana closed her eyes. "Oh, God, there were so many reasons. For a while I kept deluding myself that it would never happen again. There were good days, you know. Sometimes months passed, and then I could believe that Sam was still the wonderful man I'd married. I also didn't get much sympathy. The one time I tried talking to my parents, they sided with him. They were sure I must have deserved his anger or that I'd exaggerated it. After a while I began to believe that, too. Sometimes the psychological abuse is more devastating than the physical. Each day chips away at your self-confidence until no matter how bad it is, you're afraid to leave.

"Besides," she went on, "even if I had left, where would I have gone? I hadn't finished school. I had no marketable skills. I had no money of my own. Sam made sure I never forgot that. I halfheartedly tried hiding away some of the grocery money for a while, but he always found it. Finally I just stopped trying."

"There are shelters."

"I know that, but at the time I tried to convince myself I didn't need that. I wanted to believe that those shelters were for some other kind of woman, that if I tried hard enough I could handle Sam without anyone ever having to find out."

"What about your parents? Why didn't they listen to you?"

"They didn't want to hear. My parents were from the old school. They believed a wife made the best of whatever happened. Whither thou goest and all that. They wouldn't have taken me in."

Nick appeared shocked. "Surely they couldn't have realized how dangerous it was for you."

"No, they probably didn't. Maybe if I'd persisted, it would have been different. That's what they say now, anyway." She shrugged. "At the time, I was too embarrassed to tell them how bad it really was. They thought we were just having little spats. They never saw the bruises on my arms and legs or the gashes where his wedding ring cut into my flesh when he hit me. Ironic, isn't it, that the ring I'd given him in marriage was used as a weapon against me?"

A shudder swept through her. "Do you know once I actually went out to get a job? I thought if only I could be economically independent, I could get out. The only thing I could find was a job as a checkout clerk in a neighborhood grocery store. I took it. When Sam found out about it he accused me of trying to undermine his position in the law firm. He claimed my working in a demeaning position like that would make it seem as though he couldn't provide for me."

Her memory replayed the scene they'd had, and she drew her knees up to her chest and wrapped her arms around them as if to ward off the pain. "It was awful. He threatened to rip up all my clothes so I could never leave the apartment, and then he . . ." She swallowed a sob. "Then he saw to it that I had enough bruises to keep me from showing my face in public for a while. When I think back on the humiliation, I wonder how I lived through it."

"You made it because you're a survivor. You're stronger than you realize, Dana. After all that happened, you got out and you've pulled your life together. I wondered why you'd waited until last year to finish your master's degree. Now it makes sense. And I can see now why you would choose a place like River Glen."

He tilted her chin up until she was looking into his eyes. "Don't you see how far you've come? That's what's important. You took that experience and turned it around."

"I'm not so sure about that. Did you ever wonder why I would choose to be a librarian? I chose it because I was afraid, Nick. I was afraid of real people, of real emotions. I still am. I came here looking for a quiet, safe life. No bumps. No highs or lows, just a steady, predictable existence."

"Dammit, Dana, you deserve more than a mere

existence. Let me make it up to you for all the years of happiness you missed. You got out of one kind of jail. Don't shut yourself up in another one."

"I wish I could accept what you're offering. With all my heart I wish that I could be the kind of woman you deserve."

"You are exactly the kind of woman I need in my life, Dana. You are gentle and giving, despite everything you've been through. Perhaps even more so because of it. Tony sensed that instinctively and so did I. Don't let bitterness and fear rule you. If you do, Sam Brantley will have won as surely as if you'd stayed with him. Are you willing to give a contemptible man like that so much power over the rest of your life?"

"Nick, I want to do as you ask, but it's too soon. The scars haven't healed yet."

"Then let's heal them together. Don't go through this alone when you don't have to. Let me in. Let Tony in. We love you. We can make it easier for you."

She heard more than Nick's words. She heard the pleading tone. His eyes were shining with love. He held out his hand.

"Please. Don't fight what you're feeling for me. Accept it, build on it."

Dana hesitated, tempted. She was filled with longing, but she was also tortured by fear. She gazed into Nick's eyes, then glanced at his outstretched hand. It was trembling as he waited for her decision. Her blood surged through her, hot and wild with the promise of a new chance.

"I'll try," she said at last, slipping her hand into his. "I can't promise any more than that, but I'll try."

Nick's fingers closed lightly around hers, enveloping her in warmth. Even the roughness of his skin felt right somehow, as if it was meant to show her that strength could still be tender.

"This is right, Dana," he said, as though he had read her thoughts. He drew her close until her back was resting against his chest, where she could hear the steady, reassuring thump of his heart. "I promise you."

And for now, with summer's brightest sunlight dappling the bed and Nick cradling her in his arms, she could almost believe in the future.

Chapter 10

The image of Dana's pale, silken flesh marred by bruises almost drove Nick insane. He swore if he ever ran into Sam Brantley, he'd make him pay dearly for what he'd done to Dana. The man—no, he was less than a man—deserved to suffer tenfold the same wretched humiliation his ex-wife had suffered.

For hours after Nick had left Dana's, he had

seethed with both anger and a desire for retribution. Only the certainty that more violence would slow Dana's healing had kept him from traveling to Manhattan and going after Brantley.

Now Nick sat in his office, staring blankly at the walls. He vowed to concentrate on overcoming Dana's doubts. He would have to gentle her like a brand-new frightened filly and teach her that love could be tender and passionate, rather than filled with anger and pain. Now that he'd discovered the way it had been for her before, he would have to find new ways to prove that their love would be blessed with joy. Convinced more than ever that their relationship could be truly special, he pushed aside his mother-in-law's warnings. Surely now he knew everything.

With his goal firmly established, Nick picked up his phone and dialed the library, then tilted his chair back on two legs as he waited for Dana to answer. When she did, her voice bore no trace of the emotional turmoil she'd been through just a few hours earlier. If anything she sounded as though a tremendous weight had been lifted from her shoulders.

"I had an idea," Nick announced.

"That's your trouble," she retorted lightly. "You're always getting ideas."

"Not that kind of idea," he said, thoroughly enjoying her upbeat mood and the suggestive tone of her teasing. Perhaps on some subconscious level their talk had released her from some of the past.

"I think it's time we have some fun," he said.

"I thought that's what we'd been doing."

"Okay, more fun. Now will you be quiet a minute and let me tell you what I have in mind?"

"Certainly."

"Dancing. I think we should go dancing."

"In River Glen? Does Gracie's have a jukebox?"

"Very funny. No. I thought we'd go to Colonial Beach. There's a place there that has a band on weekends. It's lacking in decor, but it does sit out over the water. What do you think?"

She hesitated and Nick had a hunch he knew exactly what she was thinking. "Dana, you have to face people sooner or later. We really don't even know *what* they've heard. Maybe it had nothing whatsoever to do with you or your past. Whatever it is, the gossip will die down as soon as something more interesting comes along."

"When did you start reading my mind?"

"It's not all that difficult under the circumstances." He paused thoughtfully, considering something that had been bothering him. "Dana, do you have any idea how those rumors would have gotten started in River Glen in the first place? Could Sam have planted them somehow? Does he know where you are?"

Dead silence greeted his questions.

"Dana?"

"No," she said finally with absolute conviction.

"You're sure? He sounds like the kind of man who'd go to any lengths to hurt you."

"It wasn't Sam. I can't explain how I know that, but I do."

There was an odd note in Dana's voice, but Nick couldn't doubt her certainty. "Okay," he said at last, resolving to ask his mother-in-law where she'd heard the gossip. Perhaps he could trace it that way.

"Now," he said, "what about tonight?"

"If you want to endure my two left feet, it's fine with me."

"Terrific. I also thought maybe you and Tony and I would have one of our backyard picnics tomorrow. I plan to challenge you to a championship-caliber badminton game afterward."

"In this steamy weather I think croquet is more my speed."

"Maybe it'll cool off by tomorrow. Anyway, are we on for all of it?"

"As long as I get to fix the food."

"Don't tell me you're casting aspersions on my cooking, too?"

"If the shoe fits, Mr. Verone," she teased, and her tone made him smile with delight.

"Oh, it fits," he retorted, "but it's damned uncomfortable. I'll pick you up at eight."

His pulse was racing and he was filled with

anticipation as he hung up. He wasn't prepared to look up and find his mother-in-law in the doorway, a disapproving frown on her face.

"Jessica, what are you doing here?"

"I came to see you, obviously. Were you talking to that Brantley woman, Nicholas?"

His gaze hardened. He hated to be rude to her, but it was time she understood exactly where things stood. His relationship with Dana was not open for debate.

"Not that it's any of your business," he said curtly, "but yes."

"Then it's clear you haven't asked her about the rumors."

"Not directly, no, but I do have a question about them for you. Where did you hear the gossip?"

"It's not important."

"I think it is."

"Why? So you can rush out to her defense?"

"Dana doesn't need my defense. We've had a long talk and I think I have a pretty good idea what the rumors are about. I see no reason to hold Dana's past against her."

Jessica's eyes widened in shock. "You mean it *is* true! Then how can you say that?"

Nick lowered the front legs of his chair to the floor and stood up. He walked around his desk and put his hands on her shoulders. "Jessica, I am only going to say this once, so please listen very closely. I don't want to hurt you. You've always been a very important part of my life, but my relationship with Dana is none of your concern."

"It is when it involves my grandson."

"No, it isn't. If you really want to do what's best for Tony, you'll get to know Dana and welcome her into the family, because I have every intention of marrying her when she's ready."

His mother-in-law's lips tightened into a forbidding line and she shrugged off his touch. "Never, Nick. Obviously this woman has taken advantage of your good nature to lure you in, but I won't allow her to do the same with Tony. I'll fight you, Nick. In court, if necessary."

"That's an idle threat, Jessica. You have no case. I'm warning you, though, don't say one word to Tony about any of this." Nick's voice softened. "Don't you see you'll lose, Jess? Don't risk it. Don't risk losing your grandson's love."

"You've given me no choice," she said, whirling away and stalking from the office.

Nick stared after her, puzzled by her unforgiving attitude. How on earth could she hold Dana accountable for what had happened to her during her marriage? She had been the victim. Despite Jessica's attitude, though, he didn't for a moment believe she would make good on her threat. If she didn't drop the idea on her own, Joshua would see to it that she did. He was a fair man. He had already stood up for Dana once against his wife's unreasonable behavior. Nick had no doubt he would do it again, but in the meantime Jessica could make things damned uncomfortable. The only thing he could do would be to reassure Dana that she was not alone. They would face down whatever talk there was together.

With that thought, he put Jessica from his mind and began counting the hours until he would pick up Dana.

"Hey, Ms. Brantley," Tony said, pressing his thin body against her side as Dana sat at her desk. His eyes were cast down and he was chewing on his lower lip. She'd never seen him looking quite so troubled. "Can I ask you something?"

"Anything."

"How come my grandma doesn't like you? Did you have a fight or something?"

Dana felt a little frisson of fear curl along her spine at Tony's guileless question. "Why would you think she doesn't like me?"

"She was acting real weird last night. Every time I said your name she'd change the subject and Grandpa kept making these funny faces at her. I think he was mad, 'cause after dinner they were arguing in the kitchen. Grandma broke one of her best plates, too. I heard it. And then she cried."

Dana felt like crying, too. How could Jessica put Tony in the middle this way? No matter what she thought of Dana, Tony's grandmother was wrong to let her feelings affect a ten-year-old who'd already suffered too much in his young life. "I'm very sorry about that, Tony. The last thing I'd ever want to do would be to come between you and your grandparents."

She took a deep breath and forced herself to say, "Maybe it would be better if you didn't spend quite so much time at the library for a little while, especially now that it's summer and school's out."

His eyes immediately clouded over and his shoulders stiffened at what he obviously considered a rejection. "Don't you want me here?"

She put a comforting arm around his waist and squeezed. "Oh, kiddo, don't ever think that. You're my best pal. But before I came to town, you used to go to your grandparents' place every day after school, didn't you? And I'll bet you'd been spending your summers out at the farm."

"Yeah, but I like it here better. There are other kids around and you're here. Dad says it's okay with him if I come here instead. I told him I was helping you."

"And you are a big help. But did you ever think that maybe your grandparents are missing you? Grandparents are pretty special people. I never had a chance to know mine. They lived far away and they died before we could go to see them. I certainly don't want to keep you away from yours all the time."

Tony chewed on his lip as he considered what

she'd said. "Maybe I could go there some days," he said grudgingly. "And I'm staying there again tonight. Dad said so when he picked me up this morning. He said he was gonna take you out."

"Oh, he did, did he?" Obviously she was going to have to stay on her toes or Nick would be railroading her into a relationship before she was ready. She had promised him a chance. She hadn't planned to let him dominate her life. Tonight she'd make that very clear.

But that night, Nick seemed determined that there would be no serious talk. Each time she tried to broach anything important, he took her back onto the virtually empty postage-stamp-size dance floor and whirled her around until she was too breathless to say anything.

"I'm too old for this," she said, gasping as she tried to return to the table.

"You're younger than I am. Get back over here."

"I have to have something to drink."

"No problem," Nick said, sweeping her into his arms. Two artfully executed and dramatic tango steps later, they reached their table and he picked up her glass of soda and offered it to her with a flourish.

"One sip," he cautioned. "The tango is my favorite dance. I don't intend to miss a second of it."

"Why couldn't you like to waltz?" she moaned,

collapsing dramatically in his arms, an action that drew smiles and applause from the people at neighboring tables.

"Waltzing requires no energy."

"Do you consider this a form of exercise? I always thought dancing was supposed to be romantic."

"The tango is romantic."

"Two hours ago the tango was romantic. Now it's an endurance test."

"On your feet, Brantley. I didn't put this badminton net up for the fun of it," Nick said the following afternoon.

"I still haven't recovered from dancing," Dana said, lying on the chaise lounge waving a magazine to stir a breeze. She felt a little like the way Ginger Rogers must have felt after a particularly tiring movie date with Fred Astaire.

"Stop complaining, get up and serve."

She dragged herself to her feet, picked up the racket and shuttlecock. She took a halfhearted swing. The bird barely lifted over the net before taking a nosedive to Nick's well-tended lawn. He was caught standing flat-footed about ten yards back.

"What was that?" he demanded indignantly.

"A winning serve," she retorted modestly.

"Tony, get out here. Your father needs help. This woman is cheating."

"No, she's not," Tony called from the swing on the porch. "I saw her, Dad. She won the point fair and square."

"Thank you," Dana said. She glowered at Nick and said huffily, "If you're going to be a sore loser, we could switch to croquet."

"Just serve."

Dana won the game handily and turned the racket over to Tony. "Be kind to your father," she said in a stage whisper. "He's not as nimble as he once was."

"What's nimble?"

"It means his bones are getting old and creaky."

"Thanks a lot," Nick grumbled.

Dana waved cheerfully as she went inside to check on the potatoes for the German potato salad she'd promised to fix for Tony. As she plucked the steaming potatoes from the water and peeled them, she watched the badminton game through the kitchen window. Suddenly she realized she was humming and there was a smile on her face. She couldn't remember the last time she had ever felt this lighthearted. Her life felt right for the first time in years. This was what marriage was supposed to be like, relaxed and joyous with an edge of sexual tension. Yes, indeed, all the elements were there.

Lost in her thoughts, she didn't notice that the game had ended or that Nick had come into the kitchen.

"Why the smile?" he said, coming up behind her and circling his arms around her waist. His breath whispered along her neck and sent shivers dancing down her spine.

"I was just thinking how good I feel. Complete, somehow. Does that make any sense?"

He turned her around in his arms and held her loosely. "I think it does, and you couldn't have said anything I would rather hear."

Nick's gaze caught hers and she swallowed hard at the look she saw in the hazel depths. "Nick . . ."

"Don't analyze it, Dana. Just feel." He hesitated. "Okay?"

Her heart raced, thundering in her chest. Never looking away from his eyes, she nodded and he slowly lowered his lips to hers. The quick brush of velvet was followed by the hungry claim of fire. Nick's hands rested lightly on her hips in a gesture meant to reassure her of her freedom to choose between the bright flame of passion and the gentle touch of caring.

She had thought the tenderness would be enough, that it would be all she could handle, but she found herself wanting more and she stepped toward the heat. Her arms slid around Nick's neck, lifting her breasts against his chest. The nipples hardened into sensitive buds. Her hands threaded through the coarse thickness of his hair. His tongue found hers and together they performed a mating dance as old as time.

She could feel the tension in the breadth of Nick's shoulders, could sense his struggle for restraint, and that, in the end, caused her to step away.

Nick watched her closely. "Are you okay?"

"It was just a kiss, Nick."

"It was more than a kiss and you know it. It was a beginning and we both know where it's going to lead."

Her pulse lurched unsteadily, but she couldn't tear her gaze away from Nick's intent examination. "I know," she finally said in a choked whisper.

"I won't rush you, Dana. It won't happen until you're ready."

"I'm not sure I'll know when that is."

"I will," he said, and his confidence made her blood sing with giddy anticipation.

"How could you possibly double with a bridge hand that looked like that?" Nick demanded of Dana a few nights later.

"I warned you I wasn't very good."

"But any idiot knows you don't double unless you have high points in your opponent's trump suit. Did you have a single diamond?"

"I had the two and five," Dana said meekly.

Nick's voice thundered through Betsy Markham's living room. "The two and five!"

He came up out of his chair and leaned toward Dana. Instead of being frightened and backing away, she stood up, put her hands on the card table and glared right back at him. They stood there nose to nose, Nick glowering and Dana's eyes glinting with amusement.

"I warned you," she said again, relishing the newfound self-confidence that permitted her to bicker with Nick publicly without fear of repercussions.

Betsy chuckled. "Maybe I should get the peach pie now, before war erupts in my living room."

"Maybe you'd better," Nick agreed, still not taking his eyes away from Dana. When Betsy and Harry had made a discreet exit into the kitchen, Nick muttered, "Come here."

"Why should I get any closer if you're just going to yell at me?"

"I'm not going to yell."

"What are you going to do?"

"This." His mouth captured hers for a lingering kiss.

When he finally moved back, Dana caught her breath, then said, "I'll have to remember to foul up my bid in the next hand, too, if that's the punishment I'm going to get."

"That was no punishment. That was a warning. When you get to the library tomorrow, check out a book on bridge."

"Why don't you just play with Betsy as

your partner? She knows what she's doing."

"Yeah, but she's not nearly as pretty." He punctuated his comment with another kiss. "Or as sexy." And another. "Or as much fun to tease."

The last kiss might have gone on forever, but Betsy and Harry came back with the pie and ice cream.

"We'll finish this lesson later," Nick promised, earning an embarrassed blush from Dana and a wide, approving smile from Betsy.

Dana found herself humming more and more frequently as the days sped by. She no longer froze up inside at Nick's caresses. She welcomed them. She even longed for them, when she was lying in her bed alone, an aching heaviness in her abdomen, the moisture of arousal forming unbidden at the apex of her thighs. The need to have him fill the emptiness inside her was growing, overwhelming her senses.

One morning she was wandering around the library daydreaming, humming under her breath, when the aging postman came by.

"Morning, Ms. Brantley."

"Hi, Davey. I hope that's not another batch of bills."

"Don't think so. Seems like there's a couple of new books today and a couple of letters."

"Thanks. Just put the whole batch on the desk. Help yourself to something cool to drink in the back if you want to. It's a real scorcher out there again today. I'm already looking forward to fall and it's not even the Fourth of July."

"I know exactly what you mean. Back when I was a kid around here we'd go to the icehouse on a day like this and get a bag of shavings and have a snowball fight. Cooled things down pretty well. Now I'd just welcome a soda, if you have any."

"They're in the refrigerator."

When Davey had gone into the back, Dana picked up the stack of mail and idly flipped through it. As Davey had said, it was mostly flyers from the publishers. The corner of a white envelope caught her attention. Suddenly her heart slammed against her ribs, then seemed to come to a halt.

Dear God, no. Not another one.

She gingerly pulled the letter from the pile as if it were dynamite. In a very real way it was. It threatened to explode everything she held dear.

With shaking hands, she ripped it open and found another hate-filled note from Sam's parents. Her eyes brimmed with tears as she read the cruel barbs, the vicious threats. They had seemed such wonderful people when she'd met them, kind and gentle and delighted about the marriage. They had adored Sam, however, and refused to see his faults, even after all the evidence was a matter of public record.

"Dammit, no," she muttered, shredding the letter with hands that shook so badly she could hardly grasp the paper. "I won't let them do this to me. I won't let them make me go through it again."

"Are you okay, ma'am?"

Dana blinked hard and looked up to find Davey staring at her, his rheumy old eyes filled with concern.

"I'm fine."

"Wasn't bad news or something, was it?"

"No, Davey," she said, trying to put a note of dismissal in her voice.

Davey took the hint, and after one last worried glance in her direction he shuffled out. "See you tomorrow, ma'am."

Dana didn't respond. She just sank down in her chair and stared blindly at the shredded letter. Desperate to rid herself of the awful reminder, she jerked open the drawers of the desk one after another in search of matches. She knew she'd brought some in along with some candles, in case of a power outage during one of the frequent summer storms.

She finally found them in the back of the bottom drawer. She put the offensive letter in the trash can and set fire to an edge of one piece. She watched as the flame darkened the corner, then curled inward to consume the rest.

But even after the tiny fire had burned itself

out, she sat there shaken, wondering how long she could live with this torment before she shattered like a fragile glass figurine thrown against a brick wall.

Chapter 11

Nick could hear the creaking of Dana's rocking chair as soon as he turned onto her street. He'd noticed for some time that the speed of her rocking increased in direct proportion to her level of agitation.

"She must be fit to be tied about something tonight," he muttered as he slowed his pickup to a stop. He tried to glimpse her through the thick green branches of the lilac bush, but his view was blocked. She never had gotten around to pruning it back.

He approached the corner of the porch and held a paper sack up high where she could see it.

"Hot apple pie from Gracie's. Interested?"

The rocking came to an abrupt halt, but she didn't answer.

"Dana?"

"Hi, Nick." There was absolutely no enthusiasm in her voice, and a knot formed in his stomach.

He parted a couple of branches so he could get a better look at her. "Hey, what's the story? Can't you do any better than that? Whatever happened to 'How thoughtful of you, Nick,' or maybe, 'You're wonderful'?"

He saw a faint smile steal across her lips, but it vanished just as quickly as it had come. She began rocking again and that, as much as the woebegone look on her face, sobered him.

Releasing the branches, which sprang back into place, he walked slowly around the house and entered through the back. He left the pie on the kitchen counter and went straight out to the porch. He caught hold of the back of the rocker and halted its motion long enough to drop a kiss on Dana's brow. He gazed into her eyes and found the all-too-familiar sadness was back.

"What you need," he prescribed, "is a long drive in the country."

She shook her head. "I don't feel much like going out."

"Which is exactly why you should go. It's a nice night. There's a breeze stirring. We can ride along the river, maybe stop for ice cream. If you play your cards right, I'll show you my favorite place to stop and neck. We can watch the moon come up."

"I don't think so."

Nick sat down next to her and put his hand on the arm of the rocker to stop the motion again. He struggled to curb a brief surge of impatience. "What's wrong?"

When she started to respond, he held up his hand. "If you tell me I can't help, I'm going to pick you up, rocker and all, and dump you in the river."

She blinked at the lightly spoken threat, and this time her smile was full-blown. Her eyes sparkled, albeit unwillingly.

"Oh, really?" she challenged. "You and whose army?"

"You don't think I can do it?" He got to his feet, put a hand on each armrest and lifted the chair. Dana crossed her legs and grinned at him.

"Now what?" she inquired demurely.

Nick tried to take a step, but the bulkiness of his burden made movement awkward, if not impossible.

"I thought so," she said. "All talk."

"Oh, yeah?" Nick lowered the chair, scooped Dana out of it and stalked across the porch and through the house.

"Nick Verone, put me down."

"And have you think I'm some hundred-and-seventy-pound weakling? Oh, no." The back door slammed open, rattling on its hinges.

"Nicholas, where are you taking me?" Her voice rose, but it was laced with laughter.

"I told you—to the river. It's a great night for a swim, don't you think?"

"Don't you dare."

"Who's going to stop me?"

"I am."

"Oh, really?"

"Yes, really," she murmured provocatively. Suddenly Dana's lips found the sensitive spot at the nape of his neck. Nick gasped as her tongue drew a little circle on his flesh.

"Dana!" It came out as a husky growl.

"Umm?" She nibbled on his earlobe.

Blood surged through him in heated waves. His strength seemed to wane and he lowered her to her feet, letting her slide down his body as his mouth sought hers and captured it hungrily. Her arms slid around his neck and she pressed her body close to his until shudders swept through him. She smelled of lavender soap and feminine musk, and the scent drove his senses wild.

"Dana," he said softly, trying to tame the moment, but it was like trying to tame the wind.

"Hold me, Nick. Just hold me."

His arms tightened more securely around her waist and she fitted herself to the cradle of his hips, undaunted by the hard press of his arousal. Nick was caught between agony and ecstasy. Some unknown desperation had driven her into his embrace, but regret, he knew, would steal her away. He took a deep breath and stepped back.

Her eyes blinked open and she stared up at him in mute appeal. He ran a finger across her swollen lips. "Why, Dana?" he asked quietly. "Why tonight?"

A sigh whispered across her lips. "Why not?" she countered with a touch of defiance.

"Because when I walked onto your porch not ten minutes ago, you were barely speaking to me. Now you're ready to make love. It doesn't make sense."

She watched him, her expression turning grim. "Not much does these days." She regarded him wistfully. "Why couldn't you just feel, Nick? That's what you're always telling me to do."

"As long as it's honest. Can you tell me it would have been for you tonight? Or is there something you're trying to forget?"

"Maybe . . . maybe there's something I'm trying to remember." She gazed up at him, her eyes bright with unshed tears. "Can you remember what love felt like, Nick? I can't."

"Oh, babe." He swallowed hard and reached for her, but she shook her head sadly and held him off.

"No. You were right. It wouldn't have been honest. I'm not ready for a commitment and that's the only thing that would make it right."

Puzzled by her bleak expression, Nick brushed the hair back from her face and caressed her cheeks. "What happened today to put you in this mood?"

"Just a lot of old memories crowding in."

Nick held out his hand. "How about we go replace them with some new ones? That pie's still waiting."

She hesitated, but finally she took his hand and they walked slowly back to the house. They sat at the kitchen table, lingering over the pie and iced tea, talking about everything but what was really on Dana's mind.

By the time Nick left an hour later, her mood had lifted, but his was uneasy. He went home with an odd sense of dread in the pit of his stomach.

Over the next few days he saw that his fears were justified. Dana began to withdraw from him again. She could pull back without saying a word. She'd stare at him blankly and let him see the emptiness. There was a perpetual frown on her lips, and dark smudges returned under her eyes. No matter how hard he tried to learn the cause, he kept bumping into silence. After days of feeling that happiness was within their reach, it suddenly seemed farther away than ever. It hurt all the more because he had no idea why this was happening. Dana evaded his questions with the deftness of a seasoned diplomat.

A few days after his visit Nick was sitting in his study supposedly going over the company books. Actually he was thinking more about Dana's odd mood. Tony crept in quietly and came to stand behind him, his elbows propped on the back of Nick's easy chair.

When Nick glanced around, Tony said, "Can we talk, Dad? You know, sort of man-to-man?"

Nick had to bite his lip to keep from smiling.

Tony was far too serious to have his request taken lightly. He put down his pen and drew Tony to his side. "Sure, son. What did you want to talk about? Is there a problem at the day camp?"

"Nope. The camp's okay. I'm learning some neat stuff."

"That's terrific."

"It's okay." He shrugged dismissively. "But I wanted to ask you something about Ms. Brantley. Have you noticed how she's been acting kinda funny lately?"

Nick was instantly alert. If Tony had noticed, then the problem was even more serious than he'd thought. No matter how distraught she'd been, she had always managed to hide it from Tony.

"What do you mean?"

"Well, like today. I went to the library right after camp and she wasn't in front like she usually is. The door to the back was closed, but I went in anyway and she was crying. I know I probably should have knocked, but I just forgot and she was real mad at me. She never used to get mad at me, Dad."

"Maybe she was just having a bad day. We all do sometimes. Did she say why she was crying?"

Tony shook his head. "But it's not the first time. I think somebody's making her afraid."

A frown knit Nick's brow. Tony was an unusual child in that he wasn't prone to flights of fancy. He'd never had an imaginary friend or exaggerated his exploits. If he thought Dana was afraid, then she probably was, but of what?

"Why would you think that?" Nick asked. "Has she said anything about being worried or afraid?"

"Not exactly, but you remember that day I had off from camp last week? Well, I went to the library earlier that day and Davey had just been there with the mail. When I went in, she was tearing up some letter."

"Maybe it was just junk mail."

"I don't think so, Dad, 'cause she burned it."

Nick was startled and more than a little unnerved. "She burned it?"

"Yeah, in the trash can, like you see sometimes on TV. Do you think something's really wrong? I wouldn't want anybody to hurt Ms. Brantley."

Nick ruffled his son's hair, trying not to let him see the depth of his own concern. "We won't let that happen, Tony. I promise. Thanks for telling me."

Now more than ever Nick was determined to find out what was going on. That upsetting mail she was apparently getting would be a starting point. He wasn't about to give up on Dana without a fight. They'd come through too much already.

Nick made sure he was at the library day after day when the mail came. She usually left it in an untouched heap on her desk as they sat in her office sharing the sandwiches she once again automatically brought for them.

Fortunately, she didn't notice the way he surreptitiously sifted through the mail as he moved it aside, studying the return addresses, searching for something that might make an increasingly strong, always resilient woman cry. He had no doubt she'd be infuriated if she realized he was spying, no matter how well-intentioned his actions might be.

On the following Wednesday the stack was bigger than usual and Nick wasn't quite as quick. At first glance, it seemed as though there was nothing more than the familiar circulars for upcoming books, an assortment of magazines and end-of-the-month bills. Then he caught the panicked look in Dana's eyes as she spotted an envelope stuck between a farming journal and a women's magazine.

"I'll take all this," she said, grabbing for the mail. If it hadn't been for the edge of desperation in her voice, the offer might have seemed off-hand and insignificant.

Nick let her take the stack, but he caught the edge of the letter and withdrew it.

"That, too," she said, reaching for it.

"What's so important about this?"

"Who said it was important? I just want to put it over here with the other stuff." Her feigned nonchalance was painfully transparent.

Nick held the letter away from her and studied the fearful look in her eyes. Tony was right.

Whatever was in this envelope frightened her badly and she didn't want him to know about it.

"What is it about this letter that frightens you?"

"I'm not frightened."

"You are. I can see it in your eyes. You've had these letters before, haven't you?"

"Why would you say that?" The words were casual enough, but her tone was suddenly defensive. Nick knew he'd hit the mark.

"Because of the way you're acting. You're jumpy and irritable. It's not like you to snap, but you've been doing a lot of it lately."

Her eyes flashed at him. "If I'm snapping, it's because you seem to be intent on reading something that's personal. That letter is none of your business."

Nick ignored her anger. "You still haven't answered my question: have you had these before?"

"Yes, dammit! Now hand it over."

"So you can burn it?"

The mail fell to the floor as Dana shot him a startled glance. The color drained from her cheeks and her hands trembled, but she squared her shoulders and faced him defiantly. "How do you know about that?"

"Tony told me. He watched you do it. He's also seen you crying and it worried him. He finally came to me about it a few nights ago. Frankly, I'm glad he did. What's going on, Dana? Is Sam bothering you? If that's it, I'll take care of it. I'll go see him. We can get a court order, if that's what it takes."

She sank down in her chair and covered her face with her hands. Nick felt some of her fear steal into him, tying his stomach into knots.

"Dana?"

"It's not Sam."

"Then who? Is it some jilted lover who won't let go? Dana," he said softly. "Is that what it is? I can understand if there's some unresolved relationship in your past."

"If only it were that simple," she said with a rueful sigh. She glanced up at him. "After my marriage do you actually think I'd ever get seriously involved again?"

"You have with me."

"This is different. We're friends." The look she cast was pleading. It was clearly important to her that he accept that simplified definition of their increasingly complex relationship.

"Okay," he soothed. "If that's how you want to see it for the moment, I'll let it go. The important thing is these letters and what they're doing to you. Let me help. There's nothing we can't work out together."

"Not this," she said. "We can't solve this. Look what it's doing to us already. We're fighting about it."

"Sweetheart, I'm not fighting with you. I'm

just trying to figure out why you're so afraid."

"Let it go."

"No. I've already done that too often. Let me see the letter."

She continued to hold it clutched tightly in her hand. Frustrated by her stubbornness and torn by her obvious distress, Nick risked infuriating her even more by snatching the letter away from her. To his surprise Dana accepted defeat stoically once he had it in his hands. Refusing to meet his gaze, she went to the window and stared out, her shoulders heaving with silent sobs.

Now that he had her tacit agreement, Nick held the cheap white envelope with its scrawled address and debated what to do. The honorable thing would be to give it back to Dana unopened, to let her deal with whatever crisis it represented in her own way. However, she wasn't dealing with it. Rather than asking for his help, she was allowing it to eat her alive. If the stress kept up much longer, she'd fall apart.

At the image of the deepening shadows under her eyes, he made his decision. He ripped open the envelope. At the sound of the paper tearing, he heard a muffled sob. It was almost his undoing, but in the end he knew he really had no choice if he was to help her.

"I'm sorry, Dana," he said finally, relentlessly taking the letter out of its envelope.

As he read the hastily penned lines, so filled

with venom that they seemed to leap off the page, his complexion paled and his heart pounded slowly. He had no idea what he'd expected exactly, but it wasn't this. Dear God, in his wildest imaginings, he would never have considered something like this. He felt a surge of outrage on Dana's behalf even as bile rose in his throat.

At last, when he had won the fight for control over his churning emotions, his gaze lifted and met hers. Her eyes were filled with a heart-rending combination of anguish and dread.

"Is it true?" he asked, hating himself for even posing the question. His heart cried out that it had to be a lie. Yet on some instinctive level, he believed the words he'd read. They fit, like the last, crucial puzzle piece that made the picture complete.

"It's true," she said curtly.

Nick winced. He had to swallow hard to keep from barraging her with questions. She had to tell him the rest in her own time, but as he waited, he wondered if it was possible to go quietly mad in the space of a heartbeat.

He's so quiet, Dana thought miserably, watching Nick's struggle. *He must hate me now.* Then she wasn't thinking of Nick at all but of the horror of that night nearly eighteen months ago.

New Year's Eve, the beginning of a bright new year. What an incredible irony! Instead of bringing joy and anticipation, everything had ended on that night. There had been that split second of stunned disbelief, then a cold, jagged pain that tore at her insides and then, unbelievably, relief and a blessed emptiness. The guilt hadn't come until later. Much later.

And it had never gone away.

Now she looked directly into Nick's eyes and repeated quietly, "It is true. Every word of it."

She took a deep breath, then forced herself to say the words she'd never before spoken aloud.

"I killed my husband."

Chapter 12

The flat, unemotional declaration hung in the air between them. Dana had made her statement purposely harsh, wanting to shock Nick with the grim, unalterable truth. There was no point now in sparing him the ugliness.

As she had both feared and expected, his expression filled with stunned disbelief. He closed his eyes, and when he opened them it was as if he'd wrestled with some powerful, raging emotion. Finally, at immense cost, he brought it under con-trol.

"How could you?" The words seemed to be torn from deep inside him.

Her lips twisted and she said bitterly, "Sometimes I only wonder how it took me so long."

Instinctively, he reached for her ice-cold hand and caressed it, warming it. Then he released it, got up and walked away, prowling the room like an agitated tiger. Dana's breath caught in her throat as she waited nervously, watching the stark play of emotions on his face, praying for forgiveness or, at the very least, understanding.

When he finally turned back, to her amazement he apologized.

"I'm sorry. I didn't mean that accusingly, Dana. I meant that you're the gentlest person I've ever met. You couldn't even cut back that overgrown lilac bush, for heaven's sakes. I can't imagine you actually killing someone. God knows, from everything you've told me that husband of yours was sick and he probably deserved to die, but you . . ." His eyes were filled with pain and a tormented struggle for understanding.

Dana felt a new, raw anguish building up inside. She believed she was watching love wither and die right in front of her eyes. She deserved to lose his love. She'd been naive to dare to hope that with Nick things might be different, that eventu-ally they could shape a future together without his ever learning the complete truth about her past. She'd wanted desperately to believe that he would never look at her the way he was staring at her now, his eyes filled with doubt and confusion and pain.

It had been a fool's dream. Secrets had a way of catching up with you, no matter how far you ran.

Just let him understand, she thought, then wondered if even that was asking too much. The real truth was that Nick was a compassionate, reasonable man. He saw honest, open dialogue as the solution to all problems. How could he possibly accept something as cold-blooded and final as murder? Never mind that the authorities had ruled it an accidental death. She was responsible just the same. Nick would have found some other way out of a situation as horrible as hers had been, but at the time, God help her, she'd felt trapped and defenseless and more alone than she'd ever imagined possible. Her troubles with Sam had escalated far beyond the reach of mere talk.

"Tell me about it," Nick said at last. "Please. I need to understand."

Dana sighed. She didn't want to relive that night. The events that had passed still came to her all too often in her dreams, tearing into middle-of-the-night serenity to shatter her all over again. During the day she was able to keep her thoughts at bay with hard work and endless, mind-numbing chores. Now a man she loved more than anything wanted her to explain that one moment in time, that single moment in her life that had changed things forever, and had made her an eternal captive of the past.

When she didn't speak, Nick pressured her, his words ripping into the silence. "Did you shoot him, stab him, what? For God's sakes, Dana, tell me. Nothing could be worse than what I'm imagining."

The demand for answers was raw and urgent. She couldn't possibly ignore it. Why keep it from him now, anyway? He already knew the worst, and if he was ever to fully comprehend the tragedy, he had to know everything.

"No, I didn't take out a gun and shoot him," she said, feeling numb and empty. Passiveness stole over her, distancing her from everything. She tried to blank out the horrifying images in her mind and envision only the words she had to say. "God knows, there were times when I wanted to, but I didn't have the courage."

She dared a glance at Nick and found there were tears of empathy that tore her in two.

"I know this is horrible for you. I can only imagine how horrible, but I have to know it all," he said with incredible gentleness. "If I'm going to help you, if we're going to put a stop to these letters and the threat they represent, I have to know exactly what happened."

Startled, she examined his expression and saw that he meant what he said. This wasn't the curiosity or pity she'd feared. There was no condemnation in his eyes. He needed to know not for himself but for her. Only time would tell if his feelings for her had really changed as a result of what he learned, but for now he was thinking only of protecting her from any more pain. He was viewing her as the victim, not the perpetrator. It was far more than she'd dared to hope, and a wave of incredible relief washed through her.

She took a deep breath and began again. Eyes closed, she spoke in a whisper, slowly, each hesitation an instant in which she relived the devastating horror of that last night with Sam.

"You know the background. This time it all started at a party, I guess. Sam pulled me into the kitchen and accused me of flirting with some man. I don't really remember who, and it doesn't matter. It was always someone. His accusations were an excuse. When I denied everything, he pinned me against the wall and grabbed a butcher knife. He—"

She swallowed the lump in her throat. "He held it to my neck. I could feel the blade pressing against my skin."

She shuddered and clasped her arms around her middle. "Maybe it was because there were people nearby. Maybe it was just that I'd finally had too much and didn't care anymore. I don't know. Maybe I'd finally found my last shred of self-respect. Whatever it was, I screamed. I said if he ever came near me again, I'd kill him."

"And some people heard you say that."

"*Everyone* heard. They'd run toward the kitchen

when they first heard me scream. Sam let me go, tried to make a joke of it. It was an awkward moment and everyone was obviously very relieved it was over. They were glad to take him at his word. But I knew that wasn't the end. I knew things would be worse than ever when we got home."

"Then why did you go? Why didn't you stay with a friend? Go to your parents? Anything, except go home with him."

Dana laughed, the sound echoing bitterly. "Would you believe that after all he'd done to me, I was still embarrassed? I still didn't want anyone to know. Everyone loved Sam. He was a real charmer. They only accepted me for his sake. My old school friends . . . I guess I'd cut myself off from them after the wedding. I'd tried so hard to fit in with his crowd."

When Nick attempted to protest, she stopped him. "No. It was true. In his circles I was an outsider. Because of that, I was at first afraid they wouldn't believe me. And then, after it had gone on for a while, I was too damned embarrassed to admit to anyone that I hadn't left him before."

"But just that one night, Dana. People knew you'd had a fight. No one would have questioned it if you'd just asked for a place to stay until your tempers cooled. They wouldn't have had to know about the rest."

"It all makes perfect sense when you say it, but

you have to understand the syndrome. After a while you begin to feel utterly defeated and alone. You can't understand the true meaning of despair, Nick, until you've lived with it day after day, month after month. Not only that, Sam had repeatedly warned me that if I told anyone, if I tried to leave him, he'd come after me and make whoever took me in pay. I couldn't put anyone else at risk like that. And always, in the back of my mind, was that slim hope that this time would be different, that the wonderful man I'd fallen in love with would return, that he would be gentle and caring the way he was when we met. Some tiny part of me still loved that man."

She caught Nick's incredulous gaze, then glanced away. "I read something an abused woman in Maryland said not long ago. She said her marriage, her love for her husband in spite of all he'd done to her, was like an addiction. I think she's right. Making the decision to get out is no easier than kicking a drug habit or quitting smoking. All the well-meaning advice in the world won't make you leave, until you can admit to yourself that there *is* a problem."

"After all you'd been through, you couldn't admit even that much?"

"Not until that night. Until then, I had seen it as *my* failure."

Nick listened to the words and she could see that he was still tormented by the struggle to accept the twisted emotion behind them. Perhaps no one who hadn't experienced something like her situation could ever understand. She had made the only choices she could at the time, but she had learned from her mistakes. She would never again allow herself to be a victim.

"So you left together," Nick said, his tone dispassionate. It was as if he'd fought for objectivity and now clung to it desperately. "Did you fight on the way home?"

"No, the silence in the car was almost eerie. But by the time we got to our apartment, I thought maybe the worst of it was over after all."

Her lips curved in a wry grin. " 'Hope springs eternal. . . .' Isn't that what they say? As it turned out, that ride was simply the calm before an even more violent storm."

"What happened?"

"I went upstairs to the loft and began to get ready for bed. Sam stayed in the living room and had another drink. By the time he stumbled up the stairs, he was muttering jealous accusations again.

"I heard him and knew what was going to happen. I ran for the bathroom, planning to lock myself in, but he caught me. He grabbed my arm and whirled me around." Unconsciously she rubbed her arm where the bruises had marred her delicate skin for days afterward. She closed her eyes and the images flooded back.

"Sam was a handsome man, but that night his

face was twisted with fury. He was somebody I couldn't even recognize. It was a frightening transformation, as if he'd finally gone over the edge. He was beyond thinking, beyond reasoning.

"When he pulled back his fist to hit me, something finally snapped inside me for the second time that night. I woke up to the reality. I knew then that things would never change, that if I didn't get myself out I was condemning myself to an eternal hell. I was the only one who could decide how I was going to spend the rest of my life."

"And so you fought back."

"This time I fought back with more strength than I imagined I had. I hit him first. The blow wasn't much, but it was enough to throw him off balance, and I ran toward the stairs. He lunged after me."

Her eyes clamped more tightly shut as tears began to roll down her cheeks. Even with her eyes closed, the visions came back, as vivid as the night it had happened. She shuddered.

"God, it was awful. Sam was very drunk, clumsy. I shoved him back, moved out of the way."

Suddenly she was choking, sobbing as the memories flooded back. "He . . . he threw . . . threw himself at me again."

She covered her face with hands that were shaking violently. "Then—I can't remember how—then he was falling, head over heels, down the stairs. Maybe I even pushed him. I don't know. There are a few missing seconds in my mind, a complete blank. The psychiatrist says I'll remember when I'm ready."

"Oh, babe." Nick reached out to her, but she shivered and pulled away.

The words came faster now, as if by getting them all out, by telling the whole story, it would somehow cleanse her at last.

"When I came to, I was standing at the top of the steps, shaking, staring down at him, his body all crumpled, his leg stuck out at an odd angle. I thought I heard him moan, but I was terrified to go down there. I couldn't bear the thought of touching him. It must have been ten minutes or more before I finally called the rescue squad, but it was too late. He was dead."

She sighed heavily and opened her eyes. "I'd already guessed as much. The police came and they called Sam's parents in Omaha. His mother was hysterical. She had to be hospitalized. Later they made a lot out of the fact that I was so calm. The doctor said it was due to shock, but Sam's mother and father didn't see it that way. Then a few people came forward and told about the threat I'd made at the party. The whole thing blew up into a pretty nasty scandal."

"But, Dana, it wasn't murder. It was an accident. That's all, and it's over now."

She shook her head. "That's what the court

said, but it will never be over. His parents can't let it go. They've convicted me."

Her voice was flat and she stared at Nick with eyes that were empty. "And don't you see? That's not what really matters anyway, because of the way I felt."

"I don't understand."

"I was glad he was dead." Her tear-filled eyes gazed at Nick and her chin lifted defiantly. "I didn't mean to do it, I didn't mean for it to go that far, but I was glad that it was finally over. What kind of person does that make me?"

"A desperate one. A woman who had been hurt time and time again by a man she loved."

Nick's own eyes were damp and his whole body seemed to be shaking, but he took her in his arms and held her until both their trembling abated. Dana clung to him, drawing on his strength.

"Oh, babe, it's going to be okay," he promised. "It may take some time, but it will be okay."

Dana wanted desperately to believe Nick, but she'd lived through too much to believe in miracles. "You can't dismiss it that easily, Nick. Sam Brantley is dead because of me, and his parents will see to it that the story follows me wherever I go."

"There must be a way to stop them. We can see a lawyer this afternoon."

"It's too late. People here already know. I don't know how they found out, but they've obviously heard something. You've seen how I've been shunned the last few weeks. The word is spreading. It's bound to blow up pretty soon. The Brantleys won't rest until it does."

"Then that's all the more reason for us to fight back."

"For *me* to fight back, not us, Nick. It's my battle, one I'd hoped to avoid, but I'm going to stay here and fight it. I like River Glen. I'm happy with my new life. I won't let them take it away from me. I won't be victimized again."

She touched his lips with trembling fingers. "It's different for you, though. If you stay with me now, it will kill whatever chances you might have for a state or national political office."

"How can you even think about something like that? To hell with a political office, if the cost includes giving you up. Being a politician has never been my dream."

"But Betsy told me—"

"She told you that people around here think I should run for the General Assembly. That doesn't mean I've wanted to. I like what I do. Being a contractor, a father to Tony and maybe someday a husband to you—that's all I want. I have a good life, Dana. A rich, full life. I don't need to be running off to Richmond or Washington."

"If you gave that up for me, though, I could never forgive myself. It's more than enough for me just to know you'd be willing to."

"I'm not giving up anything important. Maybe if we hadn't met, I would have run for office just because it would have filled the empty spaces in my life, given me something meaningful to do after Tony's grown. But there are no empty spaces now."

Dana watched in wonder as he opened his arms. She tried to read his expression, searching for doubts, but there were none. She found only unquestioning love that sent a wild thrill coursing through her.

"Are you sure?"

"Very sure."

After an endless hesitation, she nodded and stepped into his arms.

Chapter 13

The provocative sensation of Dana nestled in his arms, drawing comfort from his embrace, her body settled between his splayed legs, stirred far more than Nick's protective instincts. He wanted her with an untimely, unreasoning desire. For weeks now he had tempered his ardor, but he could no more. His blood roared through his veins, stirring a fierce, urgent passion. A low moan rumbled deep in his throat as he tightened his arms around her.

"I need you, Nick." The tentatively spoken appeal wrenched his heart.

"You have me, sweetheart. I'm not going anywhere."

Round eyes, shimmering with tears, stared back at him. "No. I mean I really need you. I need to be with you." Her voice broke. "Please. Make love to me, Nick. Help me prove to myself that I can still feel."

His heart hammered harder. He brushed her mussed hair back from her face and studied her expression. He was searching for a hint of the fear he'd seen so often in her eyes whenever he'd openly wanted her. He understood that fear now, knew its cause, and he wanted no part in resurrecting it. If he had to wait forever for Dana to feel right about the two of them as lovers, he would.

"Are you sure? You're very vulnerable right now. I don't want to take advantage of that."

"But you do want me, don't you?"

He drew in a ragged breath. "Oh, yes. Never doubt that, Dana. I want you so badly it frightens me. I've spent weeks lying awake at night wanting to hold you in my arms, wanting to explore every inch of your body with my kisses, wanting to bury myself in you. But now, Dana? Today? I don't know."

She bit her lower lip to still the trembling. "Because of what you found out about me? Does it bother you so much?"

He ached for her and cursed himself for raising new self-doubts in her. He should have realized instantly that this had been her greatest fear of all, that this was what had kept her silent.

"No, my love. It's not that. I swear it. I don't blame you for anything that happened in your past. I just don't want you to have regrets. If we make love now, with all that's gone on today, won't you wonder later why you did it?"

She shook her head, her brown eyes never leaving his face. They shone with surprising self-confidence.

"I know why, Nick. I love you. I was afraid to admit it before today. Even if you can't love me, I have to tell you how I feel."

She rubbed an unsteady finger across his lips and they burned in the wake of that fiery, gentle touch. "You've made me feel whole again. No matter what happens between us, you've given me that and no one will ever take that feeling from me again."

She said it solemnly, with absolute conviction, and Nick felt something tear loose inside him. Doubts fled and passion rampaged more violently than ever. He wouldn't make her ask again.

He nodded and took her hand. "Let's go home."

A sweet, sensual tension throbbed between them as Dana closed the library, turning off the lights in the back, making a sign for the door announcing that it would open again in the morning. It was nothing more than routine and yet there was nothing ordinary about it. The tasks took on a heightened significance. By thc time she turned her key in the lock at last, Nick's nerves were stretched taut with anticipation.

"We'll take your car," he said, holding out his hand for the keys. She dropped them into his hand without comment.

During the brief drive to her house, he glanced at her often, still looking for some sign of reluctance, any indication that she was already regretting her impulsive declaration. He found none.

Dana met each glance with a faint smile that was almost shy in its pleasure. That look made Nick want to slay dragons for her. Perhaps, he thought once, perhaps that's what I'm doing.

When they reached the cottage, he turned off the ignition, then twisted around to read her expression again.

"Any second thoughts?"

"None," she said without hesitation. "This feels right for me, Nick."

"It feels right for me, too."

When she started to open the car door, he stopped her. "There's one more thing I want you to know now, before we go inside."

"What?"

"I love you, Dana. I don't ever want you thinking that we're here for any other reason."

He touched her cheek and repeated quietly, "I love you."

A sigh shuddered through her. "Thank you for saying that. Thank you for everything."

The walk to the back door seemed endless. Nick's sharpened senses were overwhelmed by the heavy scent of an array of colorful blossoms, the summer sounds of birdsong and bees hovering over the flower beds and the subtly provocative sway of Dana's hips as she made her way through the ankle-high grass dotted with buttercups and dandelions.

On the way, Nick plucked a pale pink rose from a bush at the side of the house. He stripped it of its thorns and tucked it into Dana's dark hair, his fingers lingering to caress the sun-kissed warmth of her cheek.

"You are so beautiful," he murmured. "This setting suits you. There's a surprisingly earthy sensuality about you."

She smiled at him and reached up to touch the rose. "Why surprising?"

"Because for so long you only allowed me to see the cool indifference, the sophistication."

"I had no choice, Nick. I was too frightened to allow anyone to get too close, especially you."

"Why especially me?"

"Because I sensed from the beginning that this day would come. Even when I was fighting you the hardest, I trusted you and I wanted you. It terrified me, because the last time I felt that way about anyone—"

"I know. You were betrayed."

"No," she said sharply. "It was worse than a betrayal. It was a mockery of what love was supposed to be."

"That's all behind you now."

She shook her head. "No. It's still very much with me, but I can deal with it now. As long as I have you, I can face it."

"You have me," he whispered, his lips claiming hers in gentle confirmation of the promise.

From that moment on, things seemed to happen in slow motion, each sensation drawn out over time until it peaked at some impossible height of awareness. Dana moved through the house in a reversal of her routine at the library, opening windows, allowing the breeze to air the rooms. When she was finished she came back to the kitchen, where Nick was waiting, his heart in his throat.

"I couldn't find any champagne," he said, holding up two glasses of apple juice. "We'll have to toast with this."

Dana took a glass, her hand trembling. But when she met his eyes, her gaze was steady, sure.

"To beginnings," Nick whispered, touching his glass to hers.

"And to the endings that make them possible."

They sipped solemnly, their gazes clashing. It

was Dana who took the glasses and set them aside. She reached for the buttons on his shirt, never taking her eyes from his. "Do you mind?"

"Be my guest."

His pulse raced as her fingers fumbled at their task. When his shirt was finally open, she touched the tips of her fingers to his heated flesh, at first tentatively and then with more confidence. Nick felt the wild pounding of his heart, the surge of his blood, and wondered just how much of the unbearable tension he could take. But it had to be this way. Dana had to be the aggressor. She had to see that with him she could be in control, not just of her own responses but of his. This first time had to have beauty and love and, perhaps most important of all, respect.

She ran her palms across his chest in a slow, sweeping gesture that set his skin on fire. When she left the matted hair on his chest and reached the curve of his shoulders, she caught the edges of his shirt and slipped it off, leaving him bare to the waist.

Her eyes lifted tentatively to meet his. "Okay?"

"Whatever you want," he said on a ragged sigh. "This is your show. You set the pace."

Her gaze swept over him lazily, and where it lingered, her touch followed so predictably that Nick could anticipate each one. The curve where neck met shoulder. The tensed muscles in his arms. The masculine nipples almost hidden

231

beneath coarse, dark hair. The flat plane of his stomach.

But if Dana's touches were predictable, Nick's responses were another thing entirely. Never had he anticipated the sweet yearning that was building inside him. Never could he have predicted the urgent hunger, the demanding need that made his legs tremble and tightened his muscles until they ached for release. Never before had he known it was possible to feel so much at the simple brush of a finger, at the fleeting touch of lips. If Dana's thoughts were bold, her exploration was still shy and all the more exciting because of it.

She sighed softly. "I've wanted to do this for so long." She looked into his eyes. "Would you kiss me again?"

Nick touched one finger to her chin, tilted her face up and very slowly lowered his mouth to hers. The first kiss was sweet and gentle. The next was an urgent claiming. His body shook with the effort of restraint. When he would have pulled away, Dana slid her arms around his neck.

"No," she cried out softly, and this time it was her passion, her hunger, that showed him the way.

"Take me to bed, Nick," she said at last. "Make love to me."

Nick scooped her into his arms without comment, his mouth claiming hers again as he moved through the hall. Dana's shoes fell to the floor. Her arms circled his shoulders and she rained kisses on his cheeks, his nose, his neck and then, at last, his mouth, lingering there for a sensual dueling of tongues that left Nick gasping.

Before they even reached the bedroom, Nick had lowered her to her feet, allowing her to slide down his fully aroused body, wanting her to know in full measure what her touch had accomplished.

"I need you very badly," he said, tilting her hips hard against him. She held back for just an instant, then swayed toward him emitting a low whimper of pleasure. "Very badly."

Dana heard the urgency in his hoarse cry and felt at first a momentary fear, then a blessed sense of triumph. This was love as it should be, demand tempered with caring, need gentled by tenderness. She caught Nick's hands and drew them to the buttons on her blouse.

"Your turn."

His fingers were much more certain than hers had been, but still she felt the trembling as they grazed her skin. She watched his eyes and in their hazel depths she saw what she had never thought to see again. She saw love. So much love that it made her ache inside. She saw her beauty reflected in his eyes, and in that awed appreciation she found contentment, a serenity that would carry her through all time.

Her blouse fell away and then the lacy wisp of her bra. Nick cupped the fullness of her breasts in his hands, rubbing the nipples with his thumb until the peaks were sensitive coral buds more than ready for the soothing moistness of his tongue. The flick of his tongue magnified the sensitivity, sending waves of pleasure rippling through her.

When he reached for the clasp on her skirt, she drew in her breath, holding it as the skirt drifted down to her ankles. She stepped out of the circle of material, then waited, breathless, as he hooked his fingers in the edge of her slip and panties together and slid them off.

When she was standing before him completely nude and open to his touch, a shudder swept through him.

"You are so beautiful," he breathed softly. "So very beautiful."

"Only with you, Nick. I feel beautiful with you."

He scooped her into his arms again and at last they finished the journey to the bedroom. When Nick lowered her to the bed at last, Dana felt as if she had finally reached the edge of forever.

She watched through partially lowered lashes as Nick removed the rest of his clothes, then stood before her in unself-conscious splendor, his body as finely tuned and well muscled as an athlete's, tanned and proud. Her lips curved into a smile and she tilted her head thoughtfully.

"I think, perhaps, you're the one who's beautiful," she whispered huskily.

The mattress dipped as Nick stretched out beside her. A smile played about his lips and laughter danced in his eyes. "We could fight about which one of us is more beautiful."

Dana shook her head. "No fighting. Not now and certainly not about that. We have better things to do."

"We do?"

She rolled toward him, feeling the first thrilling shock of having the full length of his body against hers. "We most definitely do," she said as her mouth found his.

Nick's hands claimed her with a gentleness that she blessed at first, then came to curse. She wanted more than the light, skimming, feathery touches and she urged him on, gasping when he moved from the tender flesh of her thighs to the moist heat between her legs. He hesitated until she put her hand on his and encouraged more.

An unbearable tension coiled inside her until she was pleading for release, begging Nick to set her free. Unaccountably, his fingers stilled as he insisted that she drift back to earth and join him.

Her body glistened with perspiration, more sensitive than ever to his gliding touch.

"Why are you waiting?" she asked, confused and let down.

"This is your trip, Dana. I want to be very sure we take it when you're ready."

Suddenly she understood what he was doing and she felt a swell of love in her chest. "You told me once you'd know when I was ready."

"Oh, I think you are, but it's your decision, your move."

She knelt on the bed beside him. "Now, Nick. I'm ready now."

A faint smile touched his lips as he grasped her and lifted her into position straddling him. Slowly, with the utmost care, he settled her in place. As he filled her, Dana knew a glorious instant of possession and then she was beyond thought. She was only feeling as she rode him, taking her pleasure from him. The spiral of tension wound tight again and then, like a top, she was spinning free, exultant, taking Nick with her in a burst of joy that set them both free from the past and sent them whirling on, into the future.

Much later Dana awoke in Nick's arms, feeling secure and unafraid in the circle of his strength. The bedroom was in the shadows of twilight, and in the dim, gray light, she watched him sleeping and thought again how incredibly handsome he was and how utterly right their love was.

She must have sighed because Nick's arms tightened just a little and he murmured, "What is it? Are you okay?"

"I am—" she searched for the perfect word "—complete."

His fingers ran through her hair, combing the tangles free. "You're not sore? I didn't hurt you?"

"You could never hurt me."

"I hope not, Dana."

She was troubled by his too-somber tone. She propped herself up on his chest and ran her hand along the curve of his jaw, peering intently into his eyes. "Why do you say it like that?"

He caught the tension in her at once. "Oh, sweetheart, don't look so serious. I didn't mean anything by it. It's just that it's impossible to predict whether we'll ever hurt someone. I'm sure in the beginning Sam didn't realize he would hurt you."

Dana flung herself away from him and in a voice icy with anger she said, "I don't want Sam Brantley in this bed with us, Nick. Not ever. There's no comparison between the two of you."

Nick sat up and put his arms around her shaking shoulders, soothing her until he finally heard her sigh.

"I'm sorry," she said. "I shouldn't have exploded like that. It's just that I don't want to ruin what we have."

"No. I'm the one who's sorry. I shouldn't have brought up Sam. Do you suppose we can get back to us?"

"What about us?"

"Well, for instance, are you interested in getting out of this bed and getting some dinner?"

"Dinner's an interesting option," she conceded. "But I have a better alternative."

"What's that?"

"I'll show you."

And she did. Again and again, Dana tried to show Nick just how much he had freed her from her worst memories. She replaced old nightmares with new dreams. She was fire in his arms and he was more than willing to be consumed by her flame. She took what he offered and tried to give it back tenfold, proving without a doubt the depth of her love.

Then, sated at last, they slept again.

Chapter 14

When Dana awoke, pale streaks of dawn lit the room and Nick was gone, his place in her bed already cool. For an instant she panicked, her heart thumping wildly. Why hadn't she noticed this sooner? How had she slept through his leaving?

Then she saw the note propped on her bedside table.

It's very late. You were sleeping so peacefully
I didn't want to wake you. I had to borrow

your car to pick up Tony. I'll come by for you in the morning.

Love, Nick.

"Love, Nick." She repeated the words aloud, just to hear how they sounded. They sounded wonderful. Terrific. Great. She pulled his pillow into her arms and inhaled deeply, enjoying the lingering traces of his rich masculine scent, recalling in sensuous detail his possessive branding of her body. Her flesh still burned at the memory of his wicked touch. She was Nick's now in every way that counted.

She discovered with a sense of astonishment she was at peace at last. Her thoughts were decidedly pleasant, her heart incredibly light. The past was still very much with her, but it was where it properly belonged: behind her. Nick was her present, and if good fortune remained with her, he would be her future, as well.

She bounded out of bed and scurried into the shower, filled with plans for the day, beginning with a huge, sinfully caloric breakfast to make up for the dinner they'd never found time for. She sang lustily as the water flowed over her, soothing the unfamiliar aching in her thighs. She washed her hair with her favorite herbal shampoo and then toweled herself dry until her skin glowed with a healthy blush and her hair fell to her shoulders in a damp, shining cloud that would have to wait for the taming of brush and dryer.

She straightened the tangled sheets on the bed with a smile of remembrance on her lips and moved through the house in search of stray clothing that had been tossed aside haphazardly in the night's urgency. When the last traces of their passion had been removed from everything except her memory, she began to prepare their meal—bacon, waffles, eggs, fresh-squeezed orange juice and raspberry jam. She found a vase for the rose that Nick had picked for her and set it in the middle of the table.

With an uncanny sense of timing, Nick pulled up out front just as the waffle iron hissed its readiness when she sprinkled a few drops of water on its heated surface. She threw open the back door and waited for him to turn the corner of the house. For just an instant his expression was unguarded and troubled, but when he saw her waiting there, his eyes lit up and he smiled one of his beguilingly crooked grins.

"I hope you're hungry," she announced.

"I am," he said, stealing a kiss that rocked her senses. "For you."

"In that case, you should have been here at dawn. Now you'll have to settle for breakfast."

He seemed to bristle at her comment. "You know why I had to leave, don't you?"

Puzzled by his sharp tone, she said, "Of course. You had to get home to Tony. I wasn't criticizing."

He raked his fingers through his hair. "Sorry. I suppose I'm just a little out of sorts."

Dana studied his expression more closely and saw the tiny tension lines around his set mouth, the shadows in his eyes.

"Not enough sleep?" she asked, guessing at the cause.

Nick drew in a deep breath. "Not exactly."

His mood frightened her. "What is it, Nick? What's really bothering you? Are you regretting last night?"

"No. Of course not," he said quickly, but for some reason it didn't reassure her.

"Then what?"

"Let's go in and sit down."

She dug in her heels and put her hands on her hips defiantly. "Just tell me."

He sighed heavily. "Have you seen today's paper?"

"No, I get it at the library. Why?"

But before he could respond, she knew. As surely as if she'd read each word, she knew.

"Oh, no," she breathed softly. "Is it the Brantleys?"

Nick nodded. "They sent in a letter to the editor."

He reached out to circle her shoulders and draw her close. Dana trembled violently in the embrace. "How bad is it?" she asked, her voice muffled against the warm solidity of his chest.

"It's all there. Everything." She looked up in time to see a rueful grin. "Or almost everything. I've already called a lawyer and explained the situation. He seems to think there's not much we can do. They've been very careful with their accusations. There's nothing really libelous in there. They've stuck pretty close to the court records."

"But the court declared me innocent."

"Yes, well, that's the one little fact the Brantleys didn't mention."

"You know Cyrus Mason. Will he let me tell my side of it in tomorrow's paper?"

Nick frowned. "Are you sure that's what you want to do? Do you really want to open up your past after you've tried so hard to forget it?"

"If I'm going to live in this town, I have to," she said with absolute certainty. "The Brantleys took the decision out of my hands."

"I see your point. But we'll go to the newspaper office together."

"No, Nick. I want to go alone. It's way past time I stood up for myself. Did you bring the paper?"

"It's in the car."

"Get it, Nick," she said. She felt her anger begin to build, fortifying her for the battle ahead. "I might as well see what I'm up against."

It was even worse than she'd imagined. There were innuendoes from her in-laws, unsubstantiated by police records, that she'd been drinking heavily the night of the accident. There was mention of the party, made out to seem far wilder than it was. There were suggestions that she had a history of instability, that she'd been hospitalized often for undisclosed reasons.

Facts had been taken and twisted to make a sensational story. The point? To attack her fitness as a public employee. It was the damning work of two people who had promised revenge and gotten it.

She looked up from the paper, her eyes blazing.

"They won't get away with it," she vowed. "I will not let them cost me my job, my new life."

"No," Nick said softly, his eyes shining with pride. He lifted her clenched fist to his lips and brushed a kiss across her knuckles. "This time I don't think they will."

Anxious to get on with things, she asked, "Do you still want breakfast?"

"No. I don't think either of us has the stomach for it."

"Then let me clean this up and we'll go."

She left the dishes on the table, dumped the waffle batter down the drain and slid the eggs and bacon into the garbage. Pots and pans were left stacked in the sink. Her resolve grew with every minute.

"Wish me luck," she said a half hour later as she dropped Nick off by the library so he could pick up his truck.

He grinned at her. "For some reason, I don't think you'll need it. I'll stop by the library later to see how it went."

He had started away from the car when she called him back. She touched the hand that rested on the car and gazed up at him. "Thank you."

"For what?"

"For giving me back my strength, for reminding me of who I was before Sam Brantley came along."

"I didn't do that, Dana. You did."

He leaned down and brushed his lips across hers. The kiss was greedy, but it was meant to reassure and it did. She drove away with fire in her veins and determination in her eyes.

She stalked into the *River Glen Chronicle*'s office a few minutes later and demanded to see the editor. No one dared to ask if she had an appointment. They just pointed her in the direction of a tiny, cluttered office that was littered with old newspapers and half-empty Styrofoam coffee cups.

She waited on her feet for the return of Cyrus Mason, the man listed on the masthead as editor and publisher. She paced the well-worn floor, fueling her anger and readying her arguments. By the time he came in, his shirtsleeves rolled up, his tie askew, Dana was prepared.

Apparently he was already well aware of her seething anger, because he treated her gingerly.

"Mrs. Brantley, won't you sit down?"

"You can. I don't want to." She threw the morning paper on his desk. "How dare you?"

He had no need to ask what she meant. "It was a legitimate letter," he said defensively.

"Legitimate? You call that pack of innuendoes legitimate? How carefully did you check it out, Mr. Mason? How far did you go to verify the facts? Not very far, I suspect."

"We—"

Dana didn't take note of his interruption. She never even took a breath. "If you had, you would know that I was acquitted of all charges in my husband's death on the grounds of self-defense. You would have learned that for five long years that paragon of virtue they described abused me."

Cyrus Mason turned pale. He ran his tongue over too-dry lips as Dana rushed on.

"I learned how to hide my bruises. Like a fool, I tried to protect my dignity and Sam Brantley's by keeping silent, but it all came out in court. Those hospital records they mentioned will show that I was admitted time and again to recover from the beatings their precious son gave me. Now, Mr. Mason, are you prepared to print that, as well?"

She was leaning across his desk, staring into his wide eyes, watching the beads of perspiration form on his brow. "Well, Mr. Mason?"

He swallowed nervously. "I had no idea."

"No, you didn't, did you? Isn't that your responsibility, though, Mr. Mason? Or were you afraid that the truth would ruin a sensational little tidbit for today's paper?"

"Mrs. Brantley, please, I'm very sorry."

"Sorry won't do it, Mr. Mason. This is a small town and my reputation is at stake. I want a complete and accurate report in tomorrow's paper or I will personally see to it that your lawyer spends every cent of your money defending a libel suit."

Dana knew she was bluffing at the end, but the quaking Mr. Mason did not. Perhaps he even had some sense of justice buried in his soft folds of flesh.

"I'll do whatever you like."

Dana nodded in satisfaction. "Send a reporter in. I'll do the rest."

She spent the better part of the morning with the reporter, detailing step by step the agony she had survived in her marriage. The reporter, a young girl barely out of college, had tears in her eyes when they finished talking.

"Why are you doing this?" she asked. "How can you bear to tell everyone what you suffered?"

Dana thought about the question. Until that moment, she hadn't been quite sure what her motivation was. Revenge? The salvaging of her own reputation? Or something more?

"I think maybe this is something I should have done a long time ago. Maybe by telling what I went through, it will help some other woman to avoid the tragedy of a wasted life. If just one woman reads this and finds the strength to ask for help, maybe it will give some meaning to those five years I spent in hell."

A rueful smile touched her lips as she continued. "Or perhaps I just needed to get it out of my system for my own sake, so I can move on. Maybe there's nothing honorable about my intentions at all."

The girl was shaking her head. "I don't think you can dismiss what you're doing so lightly. I think you're very brave."

"I wish I had been five or six years ago," Dana said with genuine regret. "Then perhaps Sam Brantley would still be alive."

Dana drove to the library feeling as though a tremendous burden had been lifted from her shoulders. Whatever happened now, she could deal with it. She could move on with her life. If she had a life left.

By midday she had already heard there were efforts to see that she was removed as librarian. Betsy was the bearer of the bad news.

"Dana, they've been swarming all over town hall like bees. I tried to talk them out of it, but you know how quick some folks are to make judgments. They think you're going to corrupt the young people and turn the whole town into some sort of Peyton Place. You've never heard such ridiculous carrying on."

"I think I probably have," Dana retorted mildly. "Maybe when they see the whole story in the paper tomorrow, they'll stop and think about what they're doing."

"What if they don't? Tomorrow may be too late, anyway. Some folks don't give a hang about the truth. They'd just as soon run you out of town tonight."

"What about you, Betsy? You've already jumped to my defense and you don't even know what really happened."

"Good grief, girl, I don't have to ask. I know you about as well as I could ever know a daughter of my own. Whatever happened back then, you weren't to blame. Harry believes that, too."

Humbled by Betsy's trust, Dana had tears glistening in her eyes. "How can I ever thank you?"

"You just stick around here and fight back. Don't you go running anywhere."

"I'm not running this time, Betsy. I have something to stay and fight for."

"Nick?"

"Nick."

"Oh, child, I couldn't be happier."

"Neither could I."

But even that happiness was doomed to be short-lived. Betsy had no sooner left the ominously deserted library than Jessica Leahy came in. She circled Dana's desk like a wary fighter assessing his opponent.

"I saw the paper," she said at last.

"But you already knew, didn't you?"

Jessica nodded. "I had heard something about it. Mildred Tanner's son is a lawyer in New York. He told her, and she told me right after Tony's birthday party."

For a fraction of a second there was a look of regret in her eyes, then they were a cold, stormy gray again. "Despite what you think, I didn't want to believe it."

"I think perhaps you did."

"No, Dana. I asked Nick to talk to you. I wanted you to tell him it was all lies. I didn't want it to come to this. I didn't want to be forced into a showdown with Nick."

A twisting knot formed in Dana's stomach. "What kind of a showdown?"

"If Nick persists in this craziness of his, this idea of marrying you, then I'm going to court tomorrow to ask for custody of Tony. I think after he hears this, after he sees what kind of a woman Nick plans to bring into my grandson's life, I think the judge will grant my request."

"No!" The word echoed through the room. "You can't do that. It's so unfair."

"What you did was more than unfair. You took your husband's life."

"You're wrong, Jessica." Nick's voice was icy with rage. Neither of them had heard him enter and they turned to stare at him.

"We'll see who's wrong, Nicholas," Jessica said, undaunted by his fury and not waiting to hear more. "We'll see about that."

Then she turned and left, her back stiff, her chin held high.

In her wake, she left a terrible, gut-wrenching fear.

Chapter 15

Nick slammed his fist against the wall. "Damn her for this! I warned her to stay out of it."

"You knew she was considering this?" Dana said, horrified by what Jessica Leahy was threatening and equally astonished that Nick had apparently been aware of it. "You knew she was going to fight you for custody?"

"I thought she'd come to her senses."

"Nick, you have to go after her. You have to stop it."

Nick just stood there, obviously torn between offering support to her and going after his former mother-in-law.

"Go," Dana urged. "You can't let her go into court over this. You mustn't let Tony get caught in the middle because of me. Dear God, Nick, you could lose your son."

"It won't come to that," Nick said, his teeth clenched. "I won't allow it to come to that."

"The only way to stop it is to talk to her."

Troubled eyes surveyed her. "Will you be all right?"

"I'll be fine as soon as I know you've been able to resolve this with Jessica."

Nick nodded and left, leaving Dana's emotions whirling. What if he couldn't make Jessica back down? What if she insisted on going through with the custody battle?

Then she would have to leave River Glen after all. There would be no alternative. Dana wouldn't allow herself to come between Nick and his son.

It was one of the longest afternoons of Dana's life. Not one person came into the library. No one called. By six o'clock her nerves were stretched to the limit and her stomach was churning. On the short drive home, she almost ran her car off the road because she wasn't concentrating and missed a curve.

At home she was no better. She put the unused breakfast dishes away—in the refrigerator—and washed the pots and pans with laundry detergent. Then she scrubbed the kitchen floor, trying to work out her fears and anger with each swipe of the mop. She fixed a sandwich, then threw it in the trash after taking one bite.

When the phone rang, she knocked over her glass of tea in her haste to get to it, then skidded on the pool of liquid and nearly lost her balance.

"Yes. Hello," she said breathlessly.

"Dana, it's Betsy."

Disappointment flooded through her. "Oh."

"Were you expecting someone else?"

"I was hoping Nick would call."

Her comment was greeted with a silence that went on far too long. "Betsy, what is it? Is it about Nick?"

"Nick's at town hall. They called a special meeting to decide what to do about you and your job. It starts in a half hour."

Dana sank down in a kitchen chair and rubbed her hand across her eyes. The dull pounding in her head picked up in speed and intensity.

"Should I come down there?"

"Nick told me not to call. He said you'd already been through too much today, but I think perhaps you should be here. After all, it's your fate they're deciding. You should have a chance to speak up for yourself."

"Thanks, Betsy. I'll be there in a few minutes."

When Dana got to town hall, she could hardly find a place to park. She didn't consider it a good sign that most of the town had turned out for this impromptu meeting. It had all the characteristics of a lynch mob. The phone lines must have been buzzing all afternoon. She could hear the shouts through the building's opened windows.

Reluctantly she climbed the front steps and went down the hall to the auditorium, trying her best to ignore the occasional stares in her direction. The doors had been propped open to allow for the overflow of people who were milling around in the corridor before the meeting officially got under way. Most were so busy spreading their own versions of the gossip they took little note of Dana's arrival. She slipped inside the room and stood by the back wall.

Moments later the mayor gaveled the meeting to order. It took some time for everyone to calm down. Dana saw Nick and Betsy at the front, along with the council members. Jessica Leahy was only two rows from the front, her expression grim and very determined.

Suddenly Dana felt a tug on her arm and looked around to see Tony at her side, his eyes bright with unshed tears.

"Tony! What are you doing here?"

"I was supposed to be with Grandpa, but I snuck out. I heard they were going to try to get rid of you."

Dana was stumped over what to tell him other than the truth. "That's what some people would like to do."

"But why? You can't go away, Ms. Brantley. Dad and me need you." He wrapped his arms around her waist and buried his head against her side. She could feel the hot dampness of his tears through her blouse.

Dana tried to swallow the lump in her throat and blinked back her own tears. "Let's go outside."

"No," he said, clinging harder. "I want to stay."

"No. I think we'd better talk."

She took Tony's hand and led him outside. At the moment, as frightened as she was about her own future, nothing was more important than trying to explain to him what was happening.

"Let's sit over here," she said, drawing him toward the wide concrete railing alongside the steps. He sat as close to her as he could, his thin shoulders shaking. Dana put an arm around him and sighed. "How much do you know?"

"Only what Grandma said. She told Grandpa they were going to run you out of town on a rail."

"Did she say why?"

"I couldn't hear everything. Grandpa kept telling her to keep her voice down."

Dana took a deep breath. "Okay. Let me try to explain what's happening so you can understand it."

She paused, trying to figure out how on earth she was going to do that. How did you tell a ten-year-old boy that you were responsible for your husband's death? If adults found it inexplicable, what on earth would Tony think?

"You know that I was married before?" she began at last.

He nodded. "Dad told me. He said you weren't anymore, though."

"Well, that's true. When I was married, it wasn't like it was for your mother and father. They loved each other very much. Sam and I loved each other, but we weren't very happy. Sometimes we got really angry and we fought."

"Lots of grown-ups do that."

"That's right. One night Sam and I argued and he . . . he fell down some stairs."

"Was he hurt bad?"

"Yes, Tony. He was hurt very badly. He died."

Tony seemed more perplexed than ever. "And that's why they want you to go away? That doesn't make any sense."

"Some people don't understand what really happened that night. They think I made Sam fall on purpose. They don't think a person who did something like that should be around kids."

"But you didn't mean to do it."

Dana hugged him. A tear spilled over and ran down her cheek. "No. I didn't mean to do it."

"Then go tell them, so it'll be okay." He wrapped his arms tight around her. "I don't want you to leave."

"She won't have to, son."

Dana and Tony both looked up to find Nick towering over them. She tried to read his expression, afraid to hope that his words meant what she thought.

"It's over?" she whispered, suddenly very, very scared.

He sat down next to her and took her hand. "It's over."

"And?"

"They want you to stay on."

Relief and confusion warred for her emotions. "But how? What happened? Did you convince them of what really went on that last night with Sam?"

"I didn't have to. Cyrus Mason came and brought his reporter with him. She read the story she'd written for tomorrow's paper. It was an eloquent defense."

"And they believed me?"

"They believed you."

Nick's gaze caught hers and held, and time stood still for the two of them.

"Let's go home," he said at last, getting to his feet. He put an arm around each of them and steered them through the crowd.

When they reached Dana's car, Nick touched her cheek. "I have to take Tony home."

"I know."

"I'll see you in the morning. We have a lot to talk about."

Dana nodded and watched them walk away. They hadn't gone far when Tony turned around and ran back to throw his arms around her. "I'm glad you're staying, Ms. Brantley."

She smiled at him and ruffled his hair. "Me, too, kiddo."

It was only after he'd run back to his father that she noticed Jessica Leahy watching them from the shadows. Suddenly those fleeting moments of relief and happiness were spoiled by the memory of what Jessica had sworn to do. Even after what she'd heard tonight, would Jessica still condemn her? She took a step toward the older woman, hoping to make peace or, at the very least, get some answers, but Jessica turned away.

Dana was awake all night thinking about the expression she'd seen on the older woman's face and about the threat she'd never retracted. Last night's revelations should have paved the way for her to have a future with Nick in River Glen, but now that future seemed in doubt. If, despite all the evidence, Jessica still condemned her and went on with her custody fight, then her own life here would mean very little. She wouldn't be able to bear seeing Nick and Tony parted. Nor would she be able to stay if she was forced to give up Nick so that he could keep his son.

There was only one thing to do. She had to be the one to see Jessica. She had to make at least one last attempt to make peace between the two of them.

As soon as she'd eaten breakfast the next morning, she drove out to the farm. She found

Joshua on his way to the barn. He walked over to greet her, his expression every bit as warm as it had been the first time they met.

"Congratulations, Dana. I'm glad things worked out for you last night."

"Thank you." She regarded him closely. "I suppose you know why I'm here."

He nodded. "She's inside. I think you'll find her in the kitchen. She's making bread. It's what she always does when she's got some thinking to do."

Dana could feel Joshua's eyes on her as she slowly crossed the lawn to the back door. The feeling that she had his blessing gave her the strength to go on. She hesitated on the threshold, watching as Jessica kneaded the dough, pounding it with her fists. Her anger was evident with each blow.

At last, Dana took a deep breath and rapped sharply. Jessica looked up and the two women stared at each other, tension radiating between them.

"Come in," she said at last.

Dana moved to the kitchen table and sat down, linking her hands in front of her. Now that she was here, she was unsure how to begin.

"Joshua says you bake bread when you have some thinking to do," she said finally.

"I do." The lump of dough hit the counter with a crash and flour rose like a fine mist.

"I hope you're thinking about the custody suit."

"I am." *Slam* went the dough again.

"Have you decided anything?"

"Not yet."

"Would it help for me to tell you that I love Nick and Tony very much? They are very special, thanks in large measure to the gift of love your daughter gave them. I envy the time they shared. I . . . my marriage wasn't like that. I wish to God it had been."

When she looked up, there were tears shining in Jessica's eyes. "Oh, my dear, can you ever forgive me? All I wanted to do was protect my family."

Dana got up and went over to Jessica. She put her hand on hers, oblivious to the flour and dough that covered it. She could feel the trembling and knew something of Jessica's fear.

"Don't you think I know that?" she said gently. "I can see how much you care about them, how much they love you. I just want to be a part of that, not take it away from you."

The room crackled with silent tension.

"I won't fight you," Jessica said finally.

"Thank you. That's all I can ask."

Dana was hardly aware of how long she'd spent at the farm or how late it was as she drove back to town. When she arrived at the library both Nick and Betsy were pacing the front steps, Betsy's strides only half as long as Nick's.

Betsy saw her first. "There she is," she cried, running down the steps, Nick hard on her heels.

"Where have you been?" he demanded. "We've been half out of our heads worrying about you."

"Why?"

Nick cast an incredulous look at Betsy, who shrugged. "The woman wants to know why. Good heavens, lady, after all that's gone on around here, do you even have to ask?"

"But it's all resolved now," she said cheerfully, getting out of the car. "I took care of the last detail this morning."

Nick's shoulders tensed. "What detail?"

"I went to see Jessica."

"You what!" Nick demanded.

"I went to see Jessica."

"Why?" Betsy asked. "Why on earth would you go to see her first thing in the morning?"

Nick and Dana exchanged a knowing look. She reached out and put a reassuring hand on his arm, rubbing until she felt the knotted muscle relax.

"Everything is okay."

"Everything?" he repeated as if he couldn't quite dare to believe her.

"Will someone tell me what you're talking about?" Betsy demanded indignantly.

Nick put his hands on Dana's waist and scanned her face, his expression softening. "I think we're talking about getting married, aren't we?"

"If someone asks me, we could be."

Betsy's sharp intake of breath was the only sound for the longest time. Finally Dana chuckled.

"If you don't ask me pretty soon, Betsy's going to do it for you."

"Oh, no," Nick said. "This is my proposal. Betsy can go find someone else."

"Then get down on your knee," Betsy prodded.

"Are you planning to stick around to coach me through this?" Nick inquired.

"If it'll get you moving any faster, I am."

Nick finally shrugged and sank to one knee. He glanced to Betsy for her approval. She was beaming.

"Now?" she urged.

"Dana Brantley, would you do me the honor of becoming Mrs. Nicholas Verone?"

"Can't you do any better than that?" Betsy huffed. "What did I tell you, Dana? You young folks today have no sense of romance."

Dana's heart was pounding against her ribs, and her eyes were shining as she met Nick's heated gaze.

"I think we have a very good idea of romance," she retorted softly, taking Nick's outstretched hand. "Do you think anyone would mind if I left the library closed for the day?"

"I don't think anyone would mind at all," Nick said, getting to his feet and slipping an arm around her.

As they walked away, he glanced back over his shoulder. "This part is private, Betsy."

"As long as you invite me to the wedding."

"You can be the matron of honor," Dana told her.

But when she and Nick were alone at last, she touched his cheek with trembling fingers. Her self-confidence faltered. "Are you very sure about this?" she asked, searching his eyes for signs of doubt. "My past . . . it can't be an easy thing to accept."

"Dana, you've already been much harder on yourself than I could ever be. What happened was a terrible tragedy. Not just Sam's death, but all the years of pain that led up to it. It's time now to let it go."

"I want to, Nick. God only knows, I want to." She struggled against the relentless claim of the past. "I don't know if I can."

Nick's arms encircled her with warmth and strength and love. "We can do it," he promised. "Together."

His lips met hers, gently at first, the touch of sunshine, rather than fire. It was a kiss meant to reassure. Then hunger replaced tenderness and trust surmounted doubts.

"Forever," Dana murmured, eyes blazing with life and her heart filled with the hope she'd never dared to feel before.

"Forever."

About the Author

With her roots firmly planted in the South, Sherryl Woods has written many of her more than one hundred books in that distinctive setting, whether her home state of Virginia, her adopted state, Florida, or her much-adored South Carolina. She's also especially partial to small towns, wherever they may be.

A member of Novelists Inc. and Sisters in Crime, Sherryl divides her time between her childhood summer home overlooking the Potomac River in Colonial Beach, Virginia, and her oceanfront home with its lighthouse view in Key Biscayne, Florida. "Wherever I am, if there's no water in sight, I get a little antsy," she says.

Sherryl also loves hearing from readers.
You can join her at her blog,
www.justbetweenfriendsblog.com,

visit her website at
www.sherrylwoods.com,
where you can also link directly to her
Facebook fan page,

or contact her directly at
Sherryl703@gmail.com.

Center Point Large Print
600 Brooks Road / PO Box 1
Thorndike ME 04986-0001 USA

(207) 568-3717

US & Canada:
1 800 929-9108
www.centerpointlargeprint.com